DARKWALKER 3
THE DEEP CITY

This is a work of fiction.
Similarities to persons, living or dead,
are neither intended
nor should be inferred.

ISBN: 0-9983882-7-0
ISBN-13: 978-0-9983882-7-4 (DarkFluidity)

ALSO BY JOHN URBANCIK

NOVELS
Sins of Blood and Stone
Breath of the Moon
Once Upon a Time in Midnight
Stale Reality
The Corpse and the Girl from Miami
DarkWalker 1: Hunting Grounds
DarkWalker 2: Inferno

NOVELLAS
A Game of Colors
The Rise and Fall of Babylon (with Brian Keene)
Wings of the Butterfly
House of Shadow and Ash
Necropolis
Quicksilver
Beneath Midnight
Zombies vs. Aliens vs. Robots vs. Cowboys vs. Ninja vs.
Investment Bankers vs. Green Berets
Colette and the Tiger

COLLECTIONS
Shadows, Legends & Secrets
Sound and Vision
Tales of the Fantastic and the Phantasmagoric

INKSTAINS
Multiple volumes

DARKWALKER 3
THE DEEP CITY

JOHN URBANCIK

CHAPTER ONE

1.

A pale winter sky stretches to the breaking point overhead. The road is stark and barren, the hills and mountains skeletal, and a series of brick structures loom ahead of them like the granite sentries of a graveyard.

It's a city – a town – a small town, just a series of buildings tucked away from the rest of the world. They'd left the interstate a long while back. Against the barren sky, Jack Harlow can see the cracks in the bricks, the ghosts of structures fallen or town down, and the unevenness that remains. Streams of smoke rise from a few chimneys, but otherwise the place looks dead and deserted. He asks, though there's no need, "This is it?"

"It's designed to deceive you," Lance said. "The city, what you see of it here, is an illusion."

"Some sort of magic?" Jack asks.

The road is loose gravel, but Lance's Land Rover handles it well. They're climbing uphill, but they're fairly low beneath the peaks of surrounding mountains. Jack's not entirely sure where he is, but he's never been entirely sure of anything. The road winds and dips at random, often obscuring the bricks. No one drives here. The way is treacherous. He'd enjoy testing the limits of his Mustang on a track like this.

"Not like that," Lance says. "The city doesn't look like much. There's only this one road in and out, unless you've got a helicopter, but I couldn't say when they last had one of those here."

As they get closer, the road narrows and the trees on either side crowd them. It's bumpy, slick with rain, and uncared for. Off the road, into the woods, there's still a trace of snow. There's no color in this corner of – of wherever they are. Virginia? Pennsylvania? Jack doesn't know and doesn't care. He has a friend in this city, presumably, unless Lance is lying, and Jack feels indebted.

"What do you call this place again?"

Lance doesn't answer immediately. The road requires his attention. It's early in the afternoon, not near dark, but the mountain shadows are thick and anyone would feel the eyes watching them.

They – whoever they may be – know the DarkWalker is coming.

2.

Jack Harlow, DarkWalker, did not always know what he was. He still isn't entirely sure. As a watcher, he's able to walk untouched by the things of the dark. There was one day, the worst day of his life, in which they were able to hurt him. That day, he lost his love and lover, Lisa Sparrow, to the powers of darkness. When he descended into hell to find her, he failed. He knows the things of the dark, sometimes on sight but not always immediately, but he's something more than merely a watcher. He hasn't figured that part of it out yet.

Naomi sits soundlessly in the back of the Land Rover. She's an acolyte, and he's supposed to show her something. He doesn't know what. She's more than an acolyte, too. He doesn't know what that means.

Jack Harlow doesn't know a lot. You could build cities with bricks made of his ignorance. He does, however, know Lance Turner represents the same organization his father and sister belong to. But like anything else, there are layers.

Lance doesn't answer his question, about the name of the self-proclaimed city, because a sign on the side of the road does it. *Welcome to Silver Blade.*

"It was named in the 1800's," Lance says. "Because they mined silver here."

"When did they close the mine?" Jack asks.

"Early 20's, I think." Lance shrugs. He pulls the Land Rover into a clear space in front of an inn. These streets were never paved, and maybe haven't had a car on them in most of a decade. The wood Vacancy sign hangs below wrought iron that calls the place *The Fox and Silver Sparrow.* "They're expecting us."

Jack stares at the sign. It's older than he is. It's rusted

in place. The wind couldn't move those links. He climbs out of the Land Rover.

The air is chilly but not cold. Jack's felt the ice of the deepest hells. He doesn't know if he'll ever feel cold again. Naomi, getting out behind him, whispers, "This place is old."

"You don't know old in this country," Lance says. "I don't know when, exactly, they established this mine, and this town, but it wasn't more than two hundred years ago."

"*Old*," Naomi says again.

The sun is low against the horizon. It's a high horizon line, so it's not late in the day.

"It is, however, a lot like fabled Midnight," Lance says, "tucked between the mountains so the sun never touches it. But that's primarily because this isn't the city of *Silver Blade*. This is just the mining town above it."

They take their bags and enter The Fox and Silver Sparrow. A woman behind the bar looks as old as the town. Her face is a leather mask, her eyes yellow where they should be white, the teeth still in her mouth jagged and discolored. She looks up from her book, which is also old and also leather-bound, and snarls. "You're early. We don't serve until sundown."

Lance steps forward to do the talking, which is fine by Jack. "We're expected," he says. "We have reservations."

The woman puts down her book. "You plannin' to go down, then."

"One of us, yes."

She grins. It's not pleasant to see. Jack pretends to examine the hunting trophies on the wall, instead. Is that a buffalo's head? A cougar? A bear? A many-pointed stag. He's never seen so many antlers in one place. Admittedly, he's never really looked.

Old weapons also line the walls, swords and muskets and the like, as well as tools, including a long, toothy saw that requires two people to use.

Lance is paying the woman. He's got his uses. Jack doesn't bother taking a seat. The months he spent skipping hells have diminished his absolute need for alcohol. He's not sure he'd trust the water from any spout in this place. Looking around, it's hard to see how this is a watcher facility. There's nothing here at all, and hardly any people. Outside, on the street, beyond the Land Rover, Jack sees only the wind and, on top of a weathervane that isn't moving anymore, a raven staring back at him through the dust-encrusted windows.

It's not a raven.

Even in the light of day, or the last light of a shortened day, the dark has eyes. The raven's eyes belong to someone or something.

"I don't like him," Naomi says in a whisper. "And I don't like this place. And I don't like this mission."

"It can't be worse than going to hell."

"This is no joke," Naomi says.

"We won't stay any longer than we have to. But not too long ago, I had no friends at all. And Nick Hunter, whatever else he is, proved to be a friend."

3.

Nick Hunter is the reason Jack's here.

He knows it may be a lie. He doesn't trust Lance Turner, doesn't trust his agenda, doesn't trust the people he represents. The organization. But Lance insisted Nick was lost down here, and they thought only Jack could get him out.

Jack has reservations about that *only*.

Lance returns, all smiles like they're old friends, and says, "Everything's settled. We can come down for supper in an hour. In the meantime, we're rooms four, five, and seven."

"Not six?" Jack asks.

Lance shrugs. "We're not the only guests."

"Why are there any guests?" Jack asks. "Why are there ever any guests?"

Lance shakes his head once. "Let's settle in, I'll tell you."

"You want whiskey," the woman at the bar says, "I'll get you whiskey."

"No," Jack says.

"Yes," Naomi says. "A bottle, unopened, of Kentucky whiskey, please."

"Ain't got no such thing," she says. "We got two kinds of shine, if it pleases you."

After a moment, Naomi nods briefly.

The rooms are upstairs. You go in and out through the bar of the Fox and Silver Sparrow at any hour of the day. Lance takes room seven. Naomi, carrying the smudged bottle the woman gave her, follows Jack into room four.

The small room contains a bed and a desk. The desk is big enough to hold a book. There's no chair; you sit at the edge of the bed for it. It's a twin sized bed. A musty smell permeates the room, and probably nothing will remove it. Jack throws open the window anyhow. It's all the color of sands and bark, the darker woods being the oldest bits of the place. The outer wall is brick, even inside, and lets in all kinds of cold.

"Any special purpose to the bourbon?" Jack asks.

"Thirsty." Naomi sets the bottle on the desk. "We should go back."

"To where?"

She doesn't answer that.

"It's weird, having debts," Jack says. "I still owe you a thing, I don't even know what it is."   "Neither do I."

"So you keep saying."

"How's your wounds?"

She knows damn well how his wounds are. They're fine. Her healing skills are impeccable. But the wounds his father gave the two of them hide poison inside, poison waiting to be unleashed should he, Jack Harlow, do the wrong thing. Wrong – as defined by his father. He feels the device inside him. It feels foreign. It feels dangerous.

Lance knocks and enters. "We should sleep tonight," he says, "and send you off in the morning."

"Me, by myself?" Jack asks.

"I'm unprotected. I'm merely, as you say, your handler."

"And how am I supposed to know where I'm going?"

"There's only one way to go. Down."

"And me?" Naomi asks.

"Also unprotected."

"I will not let Mr. Jack out of my sight."

"I won't stop you," Lance says, "but they'll know what you are down there."

"Acolyte, you called me."

Jack had also called her that, but it's an inefficient name. She's much more than that. He doesn't understand his own powers. He's supposed to know what a thing is, what the things are that walk the night, but more than once he's been wrong.

"Shall we drink?" Jack asks, gesturing toward the bottle of *shine*. It's not actually appealing.

Lance looks down at the bottle as if he's only just seen it. "I'll get some glasses."

"He thinks I'm weak."

"He thinks I'm untouchable."

After a moment, Naomi says, "Your friend, Hunter, why do you think he would come to a place like this?"

"Only reason he goes anywhere," Jack says. "Vampires."

4.

As night nears, the darkness over the mining town of Silver Blade grows thick. The ravens come out, and the wolves come out, but there are no wolves in this part of the country. They're not that kind of wolf. Silver Blade is not tucked out of the sunlight, but it is tucked away from the rest of the world, and it appears to have been neglected and forgotten.

Darkness doesn't prowl its streets. The darkness comes here to revel away from the concerns of the rest of the world. It's an oasis of sorts. At least, that's how Lance Turner describes it, though he admits he's never been here.

The sun has dipped beneath the mountains. Downstairs, in the Fox and Silver Sparrow, drinks are being poured, fiends and friends alike are gathering, and Jack's about to learn what it means to live in a city reserved for the exclusive use of the dark.

Someone pounds on the door to room four. After waiting a patient two seconds, they knock again. "Jack Harlow," a deep, gravel voice says. "I know you're in there. Don't make me break this door."

Naomi approaches the door. She keeps her voice low, but asks, "Who are you?"

"I will have words," the man outside says.

"And I," Naomi says, "will have a name."

The next moment stretches a long time. The door's not locked. Whoever's out there can just turn the knob. Sounds like he might be strong enough to follow through on his threat, and he's possibly not alone. Why anyone would care about Jack Harlow, however, is a mystery. He nods to Naomi, telling her to open the door. She hesitates, then pulls it open and steps back.

The man is the size of a bear, big and tall and wide and burly, and dressed in a fine, custom-made suit. He smiles broadly, opens his arms as if greeting a long-lost friend, and roars, "Jack!"

"Have we met?"

"We have now!" He thunders into the room and throws the biggest bear hug around Jack. "I know your father."

"Probably better than I do."

The man laughs. Like his smile, like everything about him, it's big and brash. "Jonathon Harlow was a good man. Mostly a good man. I would drink with his son." He glances at Naomi. "And his son's woman."

Naomi offers no response to this.

"She's not my *woman*."

"Any friend of the Harlow's," the man says, "is a friend of mine."

This, Naomi answers. "You still haven't given me your name."

"Names can be powerful things," the man says. "They call me Burke."

"You're a were-bear," Jack says, the information suddenly available to him.

"Aye, that's true," Burke says, "and a friend of your father's."

"How did you know I was coming?"

"The seer, of course."

"Seer?"

"The fortunes girl underneath," Burke says. "She sent me to fetch you, to bring you straight to her. I told her we must have a drink first, and she'd have to slaughter me to prevent it."

"Jonathon Harlow," Naomi says, "is not an honorable man."

Burke shakes his head once. "I don't know what he is now. But what he was – was simply magnificent. Come, let's drink, and toast his memory." He's already turning to head back downstairs.

"His memory?" Jack asks. "Did something happen?"

"So says your woman." Burke smiles again. It's engaging and disarming and even inviting. "He was, once upon a time, a hero, and that's the memory I would honor tonight."

"Was he here often?" Jack asks.

"Only when necessary," Burke says. "But that was long ago. Things have changed, and what was necessary once is now nothing." He waves it away. "Come. Drink."

They go.

The Fox and the Silver Sparrow doesn't take long to attract its clientele. Already, there's two dozen men and women scattered around the place, many at chairs, drinking beer and ale and mead. Lance, at the edge of the bar, has only just gotten the woman's attention and acquired three questionable glasses. He turns back to the woman to get a fourth.

5.

The old woman behind the bar runs the joint, has run it for longer than most care to remember. She brings that fourth glass to the table and sets it in front of Burke. "These are paying guests," she tells Burke.

"Brina," he says. "My sweet, lovely Brina."

"I ain't been lovely," she says, "almost as long as I ain't been sweet."

"And this," Burke says, gesturing toward Jack, "is the son of Jonathon Harlow. Have you anything to say about that?"

"I know who he is. You sure you know?"

As she walks away, Burke lowers his voice. It's supposed to be a whisper, but it still booms. "She's right, of course. She ain't sweet."

Jack Harlow watches all this and feels, like he's so often felt, that events are happening regardless of him. It's only recently that he's become so embroiled within them. Naomi is pouring drinks. She's sprinkled something into his, and into her own, and maybe she doesn't think anyone noticed. He's been a watcher for so long, he can't help but notice. She lifts her and offers a toast. "To health."

"Aye," Burke says. "We'll all be dead longer than we'll be alive."

They drink, even Lance, who puts it back like a champion. "You've been here a long time, have you?" he asks Burke.

"In Silver Blade since I was a cub. Born in the mines, I was, and my mother before me."

"We're not here about Jonathan Harlow," Lance says. He doesn't offer more.

"You don't trust me."

"I don't."

"I don't trust either of you," Jack says. He puts down his empty glass. "Tell us about this seer."

"Tania," Burke says. "You'll like here. She's red-haired and free-spirited and she's seen things in the dark you can't imagine."

Jack doesn't respond to that. "What is it you want?"

"Me?" Burke laughs. "I have everything I want."

"I don't recall a Tania in any of the files about this place," Lance says.

"Your kind ain't been around in a while. Things have changed." Burke pours himself another drink and swallows it fast. Then he rises. There's a glint of bear underneath the flesh only Jack Harlow can see. He'll be strong under the light of the moon. No one can see through these windows in the dark, not even Jack, but there's no moonlight out there tonight. Too many clouds. The moon is a week away from being full. "You'll want to go in during the day," he says. "I'll be here at dawn."

"As a guide?" Lance asks. "What do you charge?"

"Ha! Nothing." Burke glances at Brina behind the bar. "Tania wants to see you, Tania's paid my fee."

"And if we prefer to go alone?" Jack asks.

"Aye, you can try that if you wish," Burke says, nodding. "I'll be here at dawn, and you can go with me or not. I don't know yet if you're your father's son, Jack, but I'll know soon."

Lance pours another round of drinks for the three of them. "There'll be more like him," he tells Jack. "From here down to the lowest depths."

"Depths?" Naomi asks.

"Silver Blade goes deep. In the morning, you'll pass through the adit."

"And you'll wait for us here?"

"I'll remain here," Lance says, "where I'm best protected and can do you the most good."

6.

The thin walls of the inn make sleep unlikely. Jack lies on the bed staring at the ceiling. He hasn't bothered changing into night clothes. The moonshine, however potent it might be, did nothing to dull his senses. If he closes his eyes, he sees Nick Hunter trying to console him as Lisa died. It's not a memory, not a dream, but some twisted combination. He doesn't remember the last time he slept through a night.

The dark keeps many secrets, but as a watcher, Jack Harlow sees through many of them. Most of them? He doesn't know. He's not part of the organization, not yet. He doesn't want to be. In his mind, he wriggles the device hiding somewhere in his body. Not for the first time, he wonders how to defeat the poison. When his father showed it to him, he thought it was a microchip. He doesn't know electronics that well. Or poisons. If only a drop will kill him – painlessly and quickly, his father promised – there must be something that can counteract it.

The sound of the doorknob twisting interrupts his thoughts.

It's Naomi. She closes the door behind her. "I cannot sleep here," she says.

"I know what you mean."

"There's danger here."

"All sorts."

"What did you see?"

"In the bar?" Jack sits up and takes a breath. "Three vampires, two ogres, a werewolf and Burke, a bear. One troll, a satyr, and a dwarf. The woman behind the bar."

"Brina."

"Brina. She's also something, but I can't quite say what."

"Can you usually?"

"Usually."

"Are you usually correct?"

Jack hesitates. "Usually."

Naomi sits on the side of his bed with her back toward him. "You still think I'm an acolyte, then."

Jack smiles. "No."

"I believe there's hope for you, Mr. Jack," she says, "but there's no hope in this place. Why are you here?"

"My friend."

"You say that," Naomi says, "but you don't believe it. You're here for an obligation."

"He helped me when I needed help," Jack says. "Now it's my turn."

"I do not believe Lance Turner is an honorable man, either."

"What would you have me do?"

"You haven't found what you're looking for."

Jack shakes his head. "She's gone."

"She's not." Naomi turns and puts her palm on his chest. "She's here, Mr. Jack. You have to keep her with you. But this place – I fear it may steal her from you."

"I won't let that happen."

After a brief silence, she withdraws her hand and rises. "If you can't sleep, at least close your eyes and rest. Your mind will keep you going tonight, but you'll need your heart once we enter the mine."

Naomi leaves. As she shuts the door, a raven alights on the windowsill. Without even turning toward it, Jack says, "Are you here to kill me?"

The raven transforms. She's beautiful. Her amber eyes radiate the dimmest light. She says, "No, Jack

Harlow." Apparently everyone knows him. "I have something to give you." But she's a fragment of a dream, a waking dream, an image of someone Jack's never met. There's no raven in his room, no raven on the sill, but there is, in fact, a raven out there. Watching. Waiting.

Jack lays back and closes his eyes. As he pretends to sleep, he listens, and he listens more deeply than he's ever been able to before.

7.

Morning comes slowly. A diluted light makes its way into Silver Blade. The clouds are low but thin, and the sun persistent. Lance is already having breakfast with Brina, the proprietor of this establishment. The sunlight coming in through the windows is weak and pale.

"This ain't a bed and breakfast," Brina says. "You got coffee, and you got sausage. You want anything more, go kill it yourself." She disappears into a backroom.

"Are you ready?" Lance asks.

"Tell me again what to expect."

Lance shakes his head. "It's hard to say. The last person here was, in fact, your father."

"You didn't tell me that."

"Doesn't matter. It's self-sustaining. But that list visit was twenty years ago, and a lot can change in twenty years."

"How do you know Nick's down there?"

"Reports."

Jack doesn't bother with the coffee or sausage. Each looks too much like the other should. "Do better."

"One of the field reps followed Nick Hunter after your – encounter. In Orlando." He has a notebook on the table, but he doesn't need to refer to it. "Followed Nick as far as the borders Silver Blade, then called for reinforcements."

"Why would you need reinforcements?"

"Not everyone is like you, Jack. Some of the field reps are just regular people doing their job. Someone like that – someone like me – goes down into Silver Blade, they're not likely to return."

"So you call in a watcher."

"There are fewer than you would expect."

"Why not my father, if he knows this place so well?"

"Apparently, he's unavailable."

Naomi arrives. She picks up the coffee, sniffs it, tastes it, and says, "This is crap."

"It's not *akasan*, that's for certain," Jack says.

"Be polite," Lance says. "We're staying with Brina until you retrieve your friend."

"You are," Naomi says. "I won't leave Mr. Jack to face the mines alone."

Lance nods, then turns back to Jack. "There are a few possibilities, one of which you might not have considered."

"What's that?"

"That Nick Hunter has, in fact, been hunting."

"What else would he be doing?"

"If he's been hunting, you might find only death down there. This was meant to be a sort of sanctuary."

"A zoo?" Naomi asks.

Lance doesn't answer that. He's good at skipping questions. "There's also a good chance he's dead."

"When was he last seen?"

Lance glances at his watch. It's a traditional, old-fashioned, high-end thing, but Jack suspects it's a James Bond watch with gadgets and superpowers of its own. "Approximately eight-five hours."

Naomi smacks the coffee cup back down on the table. "Then we should go."

They walk through the ghost town. It's essentially that, with actual ghosts lingering in some of the corners. All the buildings still standing are brick, and all the bricks seem to lean heavily against their neighbors. They're being watched, of course, even in the straining light of dawn. Jack's been part of the dark long enough to know not all things are subjugated to the night.

Only one main road cuts through the town. The rest are alleys and lanes too narrow for Lance's Land Rover. The road leads straight to the mine entrance.

It's a low, wide mouth, with what looks like railroad tracks coming fifty yards out the front of it. The arched mouth is made up of blocks or boulders, not bricks, set as though to build a pyramid overtop. Faded paint on wood signs say *Danger* and *Keep Out* and *Enter at Own Risk.* The last of these says *Silver Blade Brothel.*

Beyond the first ten or twenty steps, the rest of the mine is carved out of the rock and supported by thick timbers that do not, in fact, promise support. But first, there's the iron gate, locked from the inside, and a man behind it with his arms crossed over his chest staring at them.

"No," the man says.

Man is not the right word. He's a troll, big enough to make Burke, the were-bear, seem small. He's got the same bleached sand color of the rock, but his eyes are brilliant blue, like the brightest beach sky Jack's ever seen.

Lance steps forward. "May I please present Jack Harlow, son of Jonathon Harlow, and representative of the organization which fosters this establishment."

Jack resists an urge to bow.

"No," the troll says again.

"It's okay," Burke says, coming from somewhere behind them. "What, you couldn't wait for me, like I suggested?" Then, to the troll, he says, "I'm here to guide him through Silver Blade to the seer."

The troll says, "The borders are closed."

"The borders are closed to *outsiders,*" Burke says, stepping closer. "I'm no outsider."

"They are."

"No," Burke says loudly. "They are friends. I shared Brina's shine with them last night."

The troll looks at Jack and seems to give this new fact a lot of consideration.

"If it helps any," Lance adds, "I'll remain up here and enjoy the pleasure of the lady Brina's company."

For a moment, the troll merely looks at Lance, looks at him as if he was a stain under his shoe. Then he laughs. It's a hearty laugh, worthy even of Burke, and the were-bear joins in. Everyone laughs, and everyone's laughing still when the troll says, "I like you, little man." He unlocks the gate. "*Lady* Brina's pleasures. I like that a lot."

"Thank you, friend," Burke says, putting a hand on his shoulder. "The lady Tania will, indeed, be pleased."

Burke enters the mine. Jack and Naomi follow. Lance offers no goodbyes. He's already walking away.

"He may not be here when we emerge," Naomi whispers to Jack.

"If we emerge."

She smiles. It's not a humorous smile.

Behind them, the troll locks the iron gate.

CHAPTER TWO

1.

Just inside the gates, a mining cart has died. It's rusted into place at the start of the tracks and will likely never move again. Once upon a time it was a wooden plank with wheels and a single handrail. The rail is mostly rust, the plank mostly rot. The troll chuckles behind them as he puts away the keys.

"It's a long way down," Burke says. "And it goes deeper than we're going."

"We're not here to see your seer," Jack says.

"She knows that. But Tania runs the joint, so you won't do anything else if you don't see her first."

At the start, there are no doors, no hallways, no variations except to follow the tracks. But around a corner, the path diverges. Burke walks as if he knows the place, which of course he does. He goes to the right, not staying with the rail, and immediately they're going down an incline. Lanterns hung overhead provide light, but only weak pools of it, and only every twenty feet or so. Jack doesn't need a lot of light to see the walls are crumbling and the ceiling barely supported by thick wooden posts that, in some instances, are cracked, rotting, or already broken.

"She's been looking forward to meeting you," Burke says as they walk. "Your father's something of a legend down here. Some of them, they think your father built this place."

"Did he?"

"Oh, no," Burke says. "The mines are older than your father, and you'll find we – our community here – is even older than that."

"Community?"

"There are two hundred free souls, last I heard." Burke rounds another corner. As they descend, the lanterns seem to dim, and offshoots hide interested eyes. Jack sees well in the dark, but not in absolute darkness, and there's nothing but absolute dark underneath the earth. He doesn't know what hides in the mine unless he sees them. All he can see are the eyes, and all he can hear are the breaths – and perhaps a hushed whisper in the dark.

"How many other souls?" Naomi asks.

Burke laughs. His sounds echo in the dark, and nothing diminishes his magnitude. "I'm sure it doesn't matter."

The tunnel ends at an elevator shaft. The nearest lantern is behind them. Only a flimsy gate prevents someone from simply stepping into the hole. Everything – metal, rock, dirt – is the same color. The elevator clanks as it rises, sounding very much like an old wooden roller coaster. It reminds Jack of going to Great Adventure in New Jersey when he was young. But this won't be anything like that.

The elevator cage arrives. It's big enough for the three of them, but Burke's size makes it crowded. He gestures them in, joins them, pulls shut the accordion style grated door, and announces, "Going down" loudly enough that anyone down there already knows they're coming.

2.

The descent is slow. The elevator seems to struggle with their weight, though Burke doesn't notice. Naomi, meanwhile, is so tense, her fists have never been so tight. There's no light in the cage itself, so there's only the dim light they're leaving above and another below. They might be passing other tunnels. The air is still and stagnant. It smells of dust and age and stillness, and underneath all that, decay. Death.

"You were born here," Naomi says.

"A long time ago, yes," Burke says. "I don't honestly remember it."

"So you don't notice the smell."

When he laughs, the whole cage shakes. "Oh, I notice it, alright."

They approach the landing. The people – the creatures – there are silent, but Jack hears them nonetheless. The breathing. The heartbeats.

They come into view of a quartet of men – things like men – armed with knives. Silver knives, no doubt. They're dogs of some sort. They all have eyes for Jack Harlow. The weapons hang from their belts.

When the cage rattles to a halt, Burke pulls open the gate and says, "I have visitors for the seer."

One of the four growls in the back of his throat. Another says, "You know the way."

The dogs fall in line behind them like a rearguard. Jack feels exposed. They march as a single unit, a single heavy footstep. That does not make Jack comfortable.

"This is the height of Silver Blade," Burke says as they descend the inclined path. "You spend your life trying to get to a higher level. You never realize there's no place to go from here but out."

The path spills into a big, open area. Columns of both rock and wood support the high ceiling – high, underground, being easily four or five stories. It stretches for a long way right and left and forward. Jack wonders that the whole thing doesn't just come down. The place is filled with huts, canvases in rows, the sounds of business and commerce.

"What are they selling?" Naomi asks.

"Anything," Burke says.

The walls are lined with ramps and stairs, and some establishments have little caverns of their own. People, and things that look like people, crowd the market. There's too many different things for Jack to register them all. Werewolves and vampires and phantasms and constructs and cambions and familiars. Burke leads them through the lane – is that the right word? – between two rows of tents, and quite a few of the creatures they pass pretend to ignore them. Others take a deep whiff as if smelling a disturbance, or openly leer, or track their progress through the market.

Burke acknowledges none of this. "The market's always open," he says. "There's always someone willing to buy, someone willing to sell."

No mere trinkets, Jack assumes. In one of the tents, he sees blades. In another, jars of color – potions and poisons, presumably.

"People want to climb out of here?" Naomi asks.

"People want to climb up to here," Burke tells her.

A man with a stump of a nose is suddenly in their path. "I have maps," he hisses.

"I have no need," Burke tells him.

"Your friends, however, will."

Burke pushes him aside – gently, almost without physically touching him. "The seer wants to see them."

"At least bring them to the arena," the noseless man calls after them. "There should be quite a show there tonight."

Jack hears the sound of a flute and the rattling of snakes and the wails of babies. He doesn't want to know. But he knows, doesn't he? How does he ignore it all?

"The seer has the best rooms, of course," Burke says.

"She sees the future?"

For perhaps the first time, Burke hesitates. He even misses a step. "She sees your soul."

Behind him, Jack sees two of the guards still accompany them, an entire discreet step back. He grins at them. They do not respond.

"Does she know why we're here?" Jack asks.

"You can ask her," Burke says. They've reached the far edge of the market. They climb two steps to get into the seer's rooms. They're curtained, and the ceilings are supported by more rotting wood. Inside, they're assaulted by the scents of jasmine and vanilla. And instead of the lanterns scattered about the marketplace, there are candles, hundreds of them, all lit, the smoke funneling through cracks in the ceiling. There are more dogs here, rippling muscles with sneers pasted to their nearly human jaws, and numerous doors, and women in veils lounging on cushions. Their lingering eyes make hungry promises. Jack realizes some of the women are boys, also in veils and wisps of silks. Their eyes make the same promises. The smell of blood is thick.

A woman runs out from the center doorway. She's human, thoroughly and completely human, but she's been heavily scarred up and down her torso and arms and face. The veils don't hide anything. Little jewels at her wrists and ankles jingle as she moves. She comes straight to Burke, stops just short of throwing her limbs about him. She offers a quick curtsey and glances quickly at both Jack and Naomi. She looks again at Naomi, perhaps sensing the scars hidden under the black woman's clothes. This woman's skin is so pale it's nearly transparent.

"The lady Tania has been waiting for you."

"What for?" Jack asks.

"She'll tell you, if she wishes," the woman says. "Please, Jack Harlow, whose father created this place, come with me."

Burke steps aside, the most subservient thing he's ever done, but Naomi steps with Jack through that center door, following the human woman into the lair of the seer.

Tania sits upon a throne. The room is tall, filled with tapestries, supported by numerous wood columns propped into place. They didn't all start out here. There are comfortable couches and beds, bowls of grapes, bottles of wine and other liquids, and three silver statuettes – a dancer, a raven, and a tiger.

Tania is not human. The throne is not really a throne, but set on a plinth it appears to be one. It's a tall, lush chair, and the woman seated there belongs in it. She's tall. Even sitting, Jack can see it. She's tall and straight and thin, her hair long and blonde, her dress gold like the summer sun. She's not human, but Jack isn't sure what she is. *Seer*, she's been called, but she sees more than just futures. She's a clairvoyant of some sort, perhaps a mind reader, perhaps one of the original Greek muses. Her human servant bows before her and announces, "The DarkWalker and his companion." Then she moves aside and takes a knee and bows her head but keeps her eyes on the visitors.

"It's rare," Tania says, her voice like music, "for someone to descend willingly. I remember your father."

"A lot of people seem to," Jack says.

"I would like to formally welcome you to the shallow city of Silver Blade. I know why you've come."

"Do you?"

"To see what your father has wrought," Tania says. But all her delicate pretty features shift as she says this. "No, you have no care for your father. You rather despise him. You're here against your will?"

"Not exactly."

"Coerced," Tania says, then turns her gaze on Naomi. "And you, you're a difficult creature to read."

"I'm a difficult creature," Naomi admits.

Tania's smile is as brilliant as all the candles. "There are deeper levels than this," she says, turning back to Jack Harlow. "You may you find you like it here. You would like it less, below."

"What do you know of my friend, Nick Hunter?"

Tania tilts her head and looks at Jack, perhaps deciding what to do with him. "Not everyone presents themselves to me."

"If there's a hunter here," Jack says, "you must know it."

"Oh, there have been many hunters. Most are dead. Three or four fought in the arena. Perhaps you'd care to join me tonight? There's to be a spectacle."

"I'm looking for my friend."

"Is that what you call him?"

"Why are we here?" Naomi asks. "In this chamber, with you, now? Why did you want to see us?"

Tania shakes her head once. "I wish to see all dignitaries. It is, shall we say, custom." She takes a breath. "I'll provide lodging, of course, for the son of

Jonathan Harlow and his companion. I'll provide food and wine. And Eulalia, my servant, shall see to all your other pleasures."

The human lowers her head even further and says, "Anything you desire can be arranged."

"We here in Silver Blade," Tania says, "are in the business of pleasure. If we go below tonight for the arena, should you change your mind, we shall have the highest balcony, of course."

And that's it. The lady Tania, the seer, is done with them. She indicates this with the minutest gesture. Eulalia ushers Jack and Naomi back out to the main room, where she curtseys again and says, "I'll show you to your rooms."

"And me?" Burke asks.

Eulalia gives him a grin. It's not an earned grin, but one that's been paid for. "You know the cost."

"I'll wait for you here."

"You don't have to."

"I serve at the seer's pleasure," Burke says. "And she has requested that I guide you."

Naomi touches Jack's arm. It says a lot. Don't ask questions. Don't make insults. Accept what's being offered, and when we're alone we can see what there is to do.

"If you would follow me, please." Eulalia opens a side door. The hall is long and curved, well lit, and lined with painted wooden doors. Red. Green. Yellow. Blue. Black. The doors are thick enough that no sounds reach the hall, but there's no question about what's happening. "This hall circles the lady's chambers. She'll be at hand if you need her. If you wish to summon me, just ring." She opens an indigo door. "I hope you find your rooms restful."

The door opens onto a broad room with a large bed, numerous chairs and couches, and a pair of veiled women draped about like finery. One is a succubus, the other a lilin. Jack doesn't know what that means, but he can make some assumptions.

"What if we'd like to explore the market?" Jack asks.

"You are not prisoners," Eulalia says. "You are free to roam as you will."

"And you?" Naomi asks. "Are you free?"

Eulalia smiles and lowers her voice. "I am happy. Is that not enough?"

3.

Jack Harlow and Naomi leave the luxuries of Tania's tent. They follow Eulalia back down the hall, because there's not much choice. Burke waits there, sprawled on a couch, one of the veiled women leaning against him and purring. He starts to move, but Jack holds out a hand. "Don't get up."

"You'll need a guide."

"We must walk alone," Naomi says, "and discuss how best to kill you when the time comes."

For a moment, Burke's eyes go wide. The purring woman hides behind him. Eulalia, elsewhere in the room, giggles briefly. Then Naomi smiles. It's not something she does often, but it's unmistakable when she does. Burke smiles, his smile grows, and then he's laughing in his typical fashion. "You are funny, you know."

"We'll come back," Jack says. "Apparently, we've been invited to the arena tonight."

"There's to be a spectacle," Naomi adds.

Out of the tent, descending the steps, entering the madness that is the marketplace, Jack says, "You don't like him much."

"Am I so easy to read, Mr. Jack?" Naomi asks.

Compared to the preponderance of candles inside Tania's cavern, the marketplace is dark. And malignant. Without a guide, without the guards immediately at their rear, Jack recognizes the depth of peril they'd walked through. All manner of darkness strolls among these tents, dark creatures birthed and raised in the dark. Jack's not stupid enough to believe his immunity makes him invulnerable. Amid the claws and talons and the teeth, he sees numerous sharp blades. Under the noise of the market, the buyings and sellings, there are growls and whimpers and the ripping of flesh.

In one tent, they sell live rodents on skewers, peeling back layers of skin to make delicate sandwiches. The rodents squeal. Bats move like battle swarms overhead, from one hole to another. The walls and ceilings are filled with cracks and crevices.

In another tent, a woman with neon green eyes examining a smoke-filled glass sphere. She looks at Jack and smiles and licks her sharp teeth.

In another tent, ghosts are tethered to objects – bones, bells, even a deck of playing cards. The proprietor hisses when he sees Jack.

At another tent, the curtains are closed, but the sign says *Get Under the Bandages*. Jack doesn't know what this means. Doesn't want to know.

"You look hungry," something says behind him.

When Jack turns, there's three of them, dogs, like the guards but without official uniforms.

One of the others grabs for Naomi's arm. "They're lost."

She snatches her arm away and meets his eyes.

"Oh, a feisty one," another says. More than three. More than just dogs. They're surrounded now.

"Oh, wait, my mistake." The dog grins. "It's me that's hungry." He grabs Jack by the arm, about to say something else, about to extend claws. He hesitates. Even here, even under the earth, even the vilest creatures tend to feel the repulsion of Jack's touch. Repulsion and pain. He's a watcher. He walks through the dark untouched, not because of agreements or covenants, but because something about him is acidic, poisonous, fatal to the creatures of the night. The dog feels it now – feels it but isn't letting go.

"Oh, my," the dog says, gripping Jack's arm tighter. "You think you're something special, then, don't you?"

"Just looking for a friend," Jack says.

The dog snarls. Others – the group around them has stopped growing, at least – laugh. It's not a friendly sound.

Naomi does one of her tricks. She slips sideways through time – Jack's seen her do it before, he's even tried it himself – she slips sideways through time and skips from where she is to the side of the dog, and she's got a hooked blade she wasn't holding before. Before the dog can react, she's got the blade pressed to his balls and is whispering in his ear. "You're not equal to this challenge."

The dog never loses his snarl, but he does release Jack's arm. "Seems to me," he says through gritted canines, "you've found a friend." Then he laughs and backs away. Naomi gives him a little nick, Jack's sure of it. He sees the movement in her shoulder.

However, the crowd doesn't really thin. Everyone wants to get a good look at the watcher. There's whisperings. "The watchers." "He's no watcher." "She's a necromancer." "He's the devil himself, returned."

This last was said by a woman in a black hooded robe. All that's visible of her face are amber eyes. "The devil himself, I say, returned from above, as promised and foretold." Others are giving them space, moving away, cowering. "You've come to deliver verdicts and vengeance, I take it. Then deliver them. Here and now. I offer myself first. Read my sins, upworlder, and pronounce my sentence." She's stepped straight up to him, and still Jack sees only her eyes. Her arms, hands, the rest of her hides under the black robes. "I demand it."

Jack shakes his head. "I don't read crimes."

"You are the son of your father," she says, "and I will have what is mine."

The sounds of the market have dimmed. Jack stares at the woman, at her eyes because there's nothing else to stare at but the black robe, and he's dealt long enough with darkness to know what can hide there. But he sees it, he really does, everything that she is – just like how he knows when a woman in a bar is a vampire, like when he recognizes a Vaudoux when he sees one. He doesn't know where the knowledge comes from, but it comes.

It must be visible in his eyes, because he can sense the change in her disposition. "Yes," she says, closer and closer still. "You see what I am, don't you?"

Jack takes a breath. He can't find his voice, so he nods. Once. It's enough.

4.

Briefly, Jack cowers. It's a real, visible thing, if anyone is looking, but maybe for a moment all eyes aren't on him. A hush grows around them, and continues to grow. The woman makes one step toward him. It's enough to send the dogs around him scurrying.

They're outside a tent selling talismans and amulets and pens and lockets. The proprietor inside, in the deepest corner, glares at them. He's a vampire, bald and blue-veined, long in the tooth and wicked in the eye, and his customers have quietly scattered, but he's not moving. He's the only one.

Even Naomi takes half a step back.

Jack takes a breath. "Are you here for me, then?"

"I've told you what I want," the woman says. "Give me my sentence."

"I can't sentence you."

"I'm guilty of much."

She's closer now, but Jack holds his ground. He asks again, "Are you here for me?"

No matter how she moves, the eyes are all he sees. If she has a nose or mouth, or a face at all, the hood and shadows obscure it. "I'm sure our paths will cross again soon enough."

"Then who are you here for?"

"Who?" She laughs. It's pleasant enough. "Sure, okay. Him." She turns to look at the vampire inside his tent.

His face is a mask of disdain and age. "If I've done anything to offend you..."

She shakes her head once. "Nothing." She extends her hand toward him. She's completely clothed in black, even under the robe, her hand a black glove and nothing more. She holds her palm upward as if beckoning him. The vampire snarls. The vampire leaps.

He doesn't reach her. His skin scorches, the flesh flakes away like ash, his muscles and tissues curl and blacken and disintegrate, and his charred bones clatter on the floor. The woman kneels, picks up one of the longer, thinner bones, perhaps a radius or ulna, strokes the edge of it, then points it toward Jack like a magic wand. "Does that satisfy you?"

"What do you want from me?"

"I await your judgement."

"I'm not the right person for that."

"Of course you are the right person. Any person can be. Today, I demand it of you, *DarkWalker*."

Naomi, at Jack's ear, whispers, "Leniency."

Jack shakes it off. Leniency would be insufficient. He takes a breath, steps toward the woman so that they're close enough to reach out and touch, and says, "I understand."

"Do you?"

"I sentence you," Jack says, taking a breath, hoping he's right, "to time served. You're free."

"You would release me?" she asks. It's almost a laugh. All around, the creatures of the marketplace, the dogs and ogres, lycanthropes, incarnate shadows, revenants, and kobolds, both push closer and pull back. None wants to miss this. None wants to be caught in the middle of it. None, not even Jack, knows exactly what *this* is.

"If I'm..."

"There is no *if*," she says. "You either have delivered my sentence or not."

"Then it's done," Jack says. "What more should I add?"

She leans closer and whispers. Naomi draws away from this, but the words are delivered straight into his mind anyhow. "Another man might have sentenced me to service."

"I am not," Jack says, "any other man but me."

Even this close, there's no face visible beneath her cloak, only those amber eyes, which seem to contain mysteries and entire worlds. "Perhaps," she says, "I'll see you at the arena."

She walks away, or fades, or simply disappears. It's hard to say. Jack Harlow doesn't move, barely manages to breathe.

Naomi says, "She was an angel of death."

"Not *an* angel of death," Jacks says. "*The* angel of death."

5.

Behind them, at the steps of Tania's curtained cavern, Burke stands with his arms crossed and watches. Many thoughts, and many questions, collide in his head. Do the others here give Jack a wider berth now, or will they mark him and, watcher or not, wait for the most opportune moment to strike?

6.

Jack and Naomi wander the marketplace, but there is nothing to indicate Nick Hunter had ever been here. There are vampires – not plentiful, but scattered, and of several different types. There are shapeshifters of all kinds.

A warlock calls to Jack from his tent. "Seeker," he says. "I can help you."

The warlock is an old bearded man. He wears no sorcerer's hat, no magical amulets of any sort, but the studded black leather favored so much by a certain type of young vampire. His knuckles are gnarled, his face cracked and rough, his eyes gray dots. "You know who I'm looking for?" Jack asks.

"You need a guide," the warlock says.

"We have a guide," Naomi says.

"I offer something no other guide will."

"What's that?" Jack asks.

"Truths."

Jack grins. "I find that hard to believe."

"I'll tell you this, and tell you free," the warlock says. "You are surrounded by creatures that would destroy you."

Jack looked around. Skinwalkers, hags, changelings, banshees, flickers, and fiends. "Thanks for the warning."

The warlock grins. "Pay me, and I'll give you names."

Jack steps into the tent. Just the one step. There's rolled parchments and silver pendants. "You called me a seeker."

"You seek a friend."

"I have a friend." Naomi remains outside the tent but close.

"You'll find him."

"Thanks."

"You'll find him," the warlock says, "but for me to tell you where, I'll need something in return."

Jack shows empty palms to indicate empty pockets. "I have nothing."

"A favor, then," the warlock says. "Not so big a thing."

Naomi, from outside the tent, says, "No."

Jack steps out of the tent.

"Wait." The warlock thrusts a pendant at Jack, a small silver thing on a silver chain. "Take this. Gratis."

"Thanks, no."

"It's a ward," the warlock says. "It will protect you."

Jack steps back into the tent and grabs the warlock's wrist. He knows how his touch feels to the creatures of the night. "I'm already protected."

The warlock stares at his wrist. "There's things that won't be so easily dissuaded."

"I'm not accepting favors."

"It's a gift," the warlock says. "Given freely. If not for you, for your woman."

"*Friend*," Jack says.

"She's just a girl here," the warlock says. "It's a wonder nothing's devoured her yet."

"Nothing's devoured anyone, that I've seen," Jack says.

"You've seen *nothing*." He spits out the last word like a curse. "You think you've descended into something, here in Silver Blade, but the shallow city runs deeper than this, and the things below – will not notice what you are until they've consumed you. At worst, you'll give them a hot shit to burn their asses."

"You talk a lot," Jack says, "but you haven't said anything."

"You haven't listened."

In fact, Jack has listened, but only to confirmations to things he already knew.

"Take it." The warlock thrusts the pendant at him again. "It is – unwise – to refuse a gift, even in the dark."

Jack snatches the pendant.

The warlock adds in a whisper, "Go below the arena. You'll see." He looks past Jack at Naomi. "You shouldn't have come."

"And you," Naomi says, "should have found a deeper hole."

The warlock grins, showing crooked, jagged teeth, and retreats deeper into his tent.

"Do you think he has information?" Jack asks.

Naomi shakes her head. "Definitely. But he only knows riddles, and he demands too high a price."

"Jack Harlow," Burke booms, approaching. "Tania would like to invite you to dinner."

"All of us?"

"You, and you alone," Burke says.

"I'll walk," Naomi says. "And listen."

"It's an honor," Burke says.

"And it would be *rude* to refuse," Naomi adds.

CHAPTER THREE

1.

Naomi moves through the marketplace like a shadow. She's quiet and swift, and she slips sideways through time to get from place to place without being observed. She knows the bear is out there, and she doesn't trust him. She doesn't trust anyone or anything down here, not even herself, not fully, and not even Jack Harlow. She watches the warlock from a distance, but loses interest when it seems he's just a man selling trinkets, a man of little power, a man who probably shouldn't even be alive.

The whole marketplace, in fact, seems rather subdued. All these creatures gathered in a single place and not tearing each other's throats out. There was the one spectacle, the vampire, but that seemed unrehearsed and unexpected.

The rest of everything here is a show.

Naomi travels from one edge of the marketplace to the other. She enters tents and stalls and looks over the things for sale. There's nothing of power. Nothing of value. There are knives, but they are regular, everyday knives, the kind you might use to cut a person but not the kind you'd use to open portals or deliver vengeance or enslave a crawler. There are pens, with which you can write, but the inks being sold are the same inks you'd find in a pen shop in fancy but otherwise unextraordinary jars. There are ghosts, yes, but what can a ghost tethered to a watch accomplish? "How much?" she asks the wrangler.

"I'm sure we can come to an arrangement," he says.

"I have money. How much?"

"Your money is meaningless to me."

"Then what is it you want?"

"Perhaps a favor," he says.

"Perhaps not."

He lowers his voice as if sharing in a conspiracy. "Perhaps they're not for sale."

"Then why have are you set up in a market where everyone is selling something?"

"Perhaps I have ulterior motivations."

"I don't like you," Naomi says.

"And I could have you killed with the snap of my fingers."

Naomi slips through time. Her blade is short and sharp. She takes his thumbs before he knows it – necessary for snapping – and takes the pocket watch. She drops it in her pouch, where she keep a great many things for a great many purposes.

The dogs – she doesn't know what they really are, why they're called that, though she has some guesses – patrol the market. They walk always in pairs, or pairs of pairs. They're big and scruffy – mutts, really – and carry blades rather than pistols. Silver blades, no doubt. Silver everything in Silver Blade, including the pocket watch. Does the silver still coursing through the veins of this mine keep most of what's down here in obedience?

Two dogs guard the elevator shaft. There seems to be no other way in or out. There are tunnels, tributaries really, but they tend to lead nowhere or turn back around on themselves. She doesn't test all of them. One may lead someplace else. Better not to wander, but to ask. She walks up to the guards at the elevator. The cage hangs there. It's old, possibly as old as the mine, but not as old as the caves beneath it. Naomi can smell the differences in age.

"What's downstairs?" she asks.

The dogs look at her. Obviously, they have no idea how to respond. They weren't prepped for this. One says, "There are no stairs."

"You're being rude," Naomi tells him.

He grunts. "There are no stairs. No downstairs. I can't help it if you ain't smart enough to ask a proper question."

She doesn't like him. In her head, she calls him Rover. She doesn't care about his real name; he's not strong enough, or consequential enough, for his name to matter. But this separates him from the rest of the pack. "What question would you prefer I ask?"

"Ask something like, what's down the elevator shaft," Rover says. His partner barely restrains a snarl. He's not well domesticated. But if they're not wolves, they're not as dangerous. Nothing here is.

"What," she says, gripping the handles of one of her blades, "is down the elevator shaft?"

"Dark," Rover says. "And silver. And screaming. And the arena."

"What's in the arena?"

"What do you think?" he asks. "Now shove off."

She starts to ask another question, but he reaches for his sword and bares his teeth. He's practically foaming at the mouth. Hasn't had his shots. His partner says and does nothing but watch, but his hand is close enough to his blade to draw it in the space of a heartbeat. She says, "Thank you," which is not something she often says – and in this case, doesn't mean at all – and walks away. No tricks. She turns her back to them and walks like anyone would walk. They don't know what she is, what she's capable of, why she's even down here.

She returns to the tent of the vampire. It's been ignored. His bones still litter the floor. She's got no privacy in this place, not really, but she's alone enough in this tent for the work of thirty seconds. She pulls powders from her pouch. Tinctures. A vial of something that smells like vanilla but most certainly is not.

2.

Jack Harlow enters the seer's lair. That's the best word for it. The setup is intimate: dinner for two, candles and jars of wine and not merely meat but fruit, fresh, from the surface. She's seated, and Eulalia is there to serve.

"I thought," Tania says, "we might have time to share a meal, and share confidences, before the spectacle."

"Confidences?"

"A game of secrets, if you will," Tania says, motioning toward the empty chair across from her. "Please. Sit."

He sits. "What kind of secrets do you expect from me?" Jack asks. "I'm a very simple man."

"That," Tania says, "is a lie."

"How are we supposed to trade secrets if you accuse me right at the start of lying?"

"No man is so simple as he seems," Tania says. "You, especially. You don't even understand yourself, do you?"

"I understand enough."

"You think you're immune to my – charms?"

Jack smiles. " I never said that."

Eulalia pours wine for the two of them.

"You've never played a game of secrets," Tania says. "I'll go first, and show you how it's done. My first secret, then: my name was not always Tania. I took it in my sixteenth year because it means queen, and I knew even then what I would be. I've always had a sort of sight, you see. Just as you have a sort of sight."

"That's a secret?" Jack asks.

She shakes her head. "My true name is the secret. Here, let me whisper it to you." They lean across the table. He feels the breath of the name on his ear.

"Cordelia is pretty, but trite, and ultimately meaningless."

She leans back. "Your turn. Tell me something equal."

"My true name is Jack Harlow. There's nothing secret about that."

"Then it's not equal."

"I didn't see anything until my seventeenth birthday."

"What was it you saw?"

"A ghost."

"There are only a few of those here in Silver Blade."

"Why is that?"

Tania shook her head. "That is not how this game is played." She sipped her wine. "I need a secret."

Jack nods. He touches the wine glass, but doesn't actually drink any. "Okay, a secret. I think you know why I'm here, and I think you're not telling me because I won't like what you say."

"That's an accusation."

"Is it?" Jack leans back. "I'm merely expressing something I haven't told anyone."

"Not even your *companion?*"

"You say that word like it means something other than what it means," Jack says.

"That," Tania says, "is your secret to keep, if you wish."

"Then it's your turn."

"Eat, first," Tania says. "There is still the spectacle."

"Is that some sort of secret, as well, that you only call it *spectacle*, and not what it really is?" Jack asks. "It's a fight. Like gladiators."

"Like boxing," Tania says, "and the feeding of lions in Rome. What else would happen in an arena? But the spectacle, there's no secret about that. It's a battle of champions. The undefeated versus the reviled. Until death."

3.

The trick is speed and agility. The dogs stand guard over the elevator, and no one, as Naomi watches, uses it. The cage hangs still. The controls rot and rust in silence.

Do they smell her? Maybe. But they can't see her, and they can't hear her, and she's already been here so perhaps her scent lingers. She doubts they're that stupid. But they are, in fact, that stupid. She doesn't get too close, doesn't get close enough that they could skewer her with their silver blades.

Everything in Silver Blade is silver, wood, or rock.

Naomi slips past them. Her stealth won't last long, so she must be quick. She slips past the guards, around the edge of the cage, and into the shaft. She only barely touches the cage but it's enough to cause it to shudder. Still, the dogs see nothing.

Naomi holds her breath, and she clings to the side of the rock wall. It's rough, so there are handholds. It's a small cage and a small hole. She descends, hand under hand, foot under foot. Climbing was never her specialty, but despite that this is a straight drop, this isn't the most difficult descent. She climbs down into darkness, into the source of many scents, many other scents, nothing like the marketplace.

Silver Blade is too clean.

Naomi reaches the next landing. Four dogs sit around a table playing cards, their weapons at the ready, snarling at each other, playing for chunks of sulfur and arsenic. All as one, they look at the elevator shaft, at whatever thinnest sound Naomi must've made, but there's no sign of movement, no indication the elevator is descending. They return to their game.

She slips past them, sideways through time, one of the earliest little tricks she ever learned and still so very useful. The descent was fifty yards or more, difficult, tiring, but there's no time to rest.

This cave isn't like above. It's dark, more crowded, lined by a set of old railway tracks. It doesn't lead to another big cavern, but to numerous little caves, tendrils snaking off into the rock. Some of the doors are locked. Some of the locked doors have barred windows to look through. Some of those windows look in on nothing and no one, empty little cells, while others hold prisoners of some sort, various creatures less human in appearance than anything in the marketplace.

It's a labyrinth, of course, and in any such maze there are monsters. She finds a dried and desiccated corpse nailed to the rock wall with silver spikes through its wrists and belly. Its eyes have long since gone, and its bones look brittle like chalk. Even still, it sees her, and its head turns as she passes, and the sound echoes through the corridors.

The caves incline or decline seemingly at random. At every juncture, she looks left and right, up and down, straight ahead and back, listening for indications, looking for any sign of anything. There are pits and holes. These were manmade tunnels, mostly, supported by thick rotting timbers. Properly, they're mineshafts, not caves, and they seem to stretch in every direction.

In one place, she finds three hunched creatures sharing a fire. It's the brightest light she's seen. They're eating meat, raw, off the corpse of something else, eating noisily and sloppily, laughing nasally, beady little eyes and bald little heads. They suck the blood off the bones and smack their lips.

She slips past them.

In another place, a dead end corridor, Naomi finds a woman pacing, ranting in a language Naomi recognizes only as old, to a trio of cowering servants. The woman is old, too, her skin translucent, the blood in her veins iridescent green. She stops suddenly to look directly at Naomi, snarling and slathering, and gives a command.

The servants – no, pets – all turn.

Naomi slips backwards. The servants lope after her. Their claws clatter on the rock floor. Their eyes glow the same green as the woman's blood.

Naomi slips to a crossroads, but they're not far behind her. She slips sideways down one, then sideways down the other, then makes herself as small and invisible as possible. She uses the mixture she'd prepared in the marketplace to mask herself. The rock seems to enclose her.

The servants reach the crossroads. Behind them, the woman shouts more commands. Naomi hears chains clanging back there. Had the woman been bound?

The servants are. Their leashes won't allow them beyond the crossroads. Naomi's choice of cover is just within their reach. They must know every corner of their limits, every crack and crevice. They snarl down one corridor and another, and turn toward the changes in their environment.

The green-veined woman steps out of the cave. She holds the chains. The woman asks something as she approaches Naomi.

Naomi attempts to slip sideways, but the woman catches her by the wrist. Naomi draws one of her blades, but the woman catches her other wrist. Her iron grip is unbreakable. She asks again, and Naomi says, "I don't understand you."

The woman says something else and laughs, then locks a cuff around Naomi's wrist.

4.

"Another secret," Tania says, finishing her wine. Even as she puts the glass down, Eulalia is there to refill it. "You go first this time."

"I don't enjoy games," Jack says.

Tania shakes her head. "However," she says, "you are, at your heart, a seeker of truths, an exposer of secrets, a man who wishes to know the unknown. Isn't that right?" When he doesn't immediately answer, she says, "Of course I'm right. That's why you're here, in Silver Blade, playing at being an explorer. That's why they chose you."

"Chose me?"

"It's why you pretend to be a watcher," Tania says. "So you can watch and learn and know. You would know everything, if you could. And you would keep your secrets."

Jack doesn't respond to that. He says, "If you know why I'm here, why all these games? Tell me what I want to know."

"What you think you want to know?" Tania asks. "Or what you really want to know?" She beckons Eulalia, who quickly and quietly appears at her side. "You want to know why this girl is still alive in this place, where monsters wander the halls."

"I haven't seen halls," Jack says.

"There's much you haven't seen. You want to know how she got these scars."

He glances at Eulalia, who meets his eye.

"You want to know whether I gave them to her, or if I saved her from someone else. You want to know why she's in service to me. Your curiosity is positively seething."

After a moment, Jack returns his gaze to Tania. "I don't really care. Not about her, not about you, not about this place."

"And yet here you are."

Abruptly, Jack stands, pushing the chair back and jostling the table. The silverware clinks. The wine in its glass sloshes over the edge. Drops land redly on the white tablecloth. Eulalia gasps and steps away. Tania is on her feet. "I have been nothing but hospitable to you."

"You have told me nothing but lies," Jack says. "Where is my friend? Where is Nick Hunter?"

Tania shakes her head. She dabs her lips with a cloth napkin. "But I've been telling you this whole time, Jack Harlow. Your friend is part of the spectacle."

5.

The spectacle takes places in an arena underneath the highest layers of Silver Blade. Thousands of seats surround a stage – where the event will take place. In another place, it might very well be a rock band with lasers and smoke machines and stacks of speakers. In yet another place, it might be Roman gladiators. Here, it's to be the undefeated and the reviled.

Once upon a time, the reviled walked the earth and sent many creatures to their doom. He, and no one else, decided what condemned a creature to death and what made it innocent.

The undefeated has never lost.

The two have never met. When they do, one will die.

There is, however, no audience of thousands. In the dark, there are a dozen spectators scattered amongst the stands, sitting in the stone. Tania, as seer, commands the highest of balconies. Jack Harlow sits beside her, but he's not a willing participant and he's not there by choice. His wrists are bound. The scarred Eulalia stands behind him. She has knives.

"There's never been a hunter in Silver Blade," Tania says. "They were denied the shallow city so that we might flourish. Your father did that, not so very long ago. But even before that, they weren't foolish enough to enter the lair. They drew a line. You stay underground, we'll stay overhead. I bet you've been to their town. Since the 1800s, they've been up there, pretending to keep watch over these mines. But they're not merely mines, Jack Harlow."

The floor of the arena is rock smoothed by time and friction. Jack can see blood where former champions fell. The ground is smoothed, but also scratched, gouged, bleeding. It's not silver, but sliver-like, something Jack doesn't recognize.

"They built the mines, Jack Harlow. They tapped into the very heart of the mountain. They excavated, and in the beginning, in the beginning days of the shallow city, they sought to make slaves of the wolves. There were some battles, I can tell you that. But war? There's never been a war."

The arena is mostly shrouded in darkness, stands and fighting floor alike. Fires in cauldrons provide some light, but it makes little difference. There are shadows down here, and mists in the shadows, and elemental things within those mists. There is dust, but there is no great crowd to watch it.

"One day, perhaps, war will come," Tania says, turning to look at Jack again. "I'm afraid I'm not a seer of futures. I cannot say."

In the stands, making up an audience of dozens in an arena built for thousands, there are vampires and dogs – dogs who were once wolves, or descended from wolves, once enslaved to work these mines. There are spirits and the echoes of spirits. There are vampire merchants and shapeshifters and all the creatures of the marketplace – even the angel of death herself, all the way on the other side of the arena, whose yellow eyes are as bright as any of the fires.

"There will, however, be death this day," Tania says. "I'm afraid, in Silver Blade, most days bring death of some sort."

"This is the spectacle?" Jack Harlow asks. "An empty arena carved out of the earth?"

"It is something to see, though, wouldn't you say?" Tania gestures toward the corners. "Look, and you'll see the timbers holding the earth over this city. Do you see how the wood rots and trembles before our eyes? It's a slow process, it may take years or centuries, it may not happen until after I've died, but one day that ceiling will come crashing down on us and bury this city, the shallow and the deep, forever. That's why you're here, isn't it? To see if the city can still stand? To see if the balustrades still hold?" She turns on him again, smiling, and he sees for the first time the sharpness of her teeth and eyes. "There are only two directions in Silver Blade. Up, and down. The arena is down. Below that, the warriors sleep, and below that there are slaves and miners still pulling silver out of the mountain, silver and all the other great riches underground. But there's one direction not available to us, Jack Harlow, not to me and not to you. There's no *out.*"

Jack smiles. It's not the response she expects. He says, "I've escaped a hundred hells. I don't think your city can hold me."

"We've all said such words," Tania tells him. "We've all failed."

Somewhere, someone bangs a gong. The brass sound echoes the full length of the arena. The one strike signals the beginning of the match. A stone door slides open. The reviled is prodded forward. Nick Hunter, dirty bloodied blonde hair, limps onto the stone field. He carries knives and swords and guns, as promised, but wears no armor.

The undefeated has already been in the arena. The undefeated has been in the marketplace and in the comfortable rooms Tania had offered. The undefeated has dined at her table, and at all tables, if there are any tables to be had. The undefeated is not a great beast or a small creature or a knight or assassin. The undefeated is time, time and weight, the weight of the earth crushing

Silver Blade beneath it, the weight of ages. Nick Hunter, already tortured, already bruised and beaten, stands a dozen steps from the wall waiting for an opponent to enter the arena and face him. He's fought vampires. He's faced zombies and wraiths and demons. He stood beside Jack Harlow at his darkest hour. And now he stands alone, he cannot from that distance see Jack in the balcony or any particular person. He can see the stains of past warriors who have failed against the undefeated. He can see the dust on the rock floor is ground up bone.

Tania smiles. Even Eulalia steps forward, so that her leg touches the side of Jack as she peers over the balcony edge.

"How long do you think he will last?" Tania asks.

6.

Nick Hunter stands in the arena awaiting his fate. He doesn't know what he'll face. He imagines it'll be even more horrible than the things he's already fought. Always a vampire hunter, since the day one of those foul things came out of the earth and slaughtered his friends and family. Only a vampire hunter until the day he learned what else hid in the dark. He's spent the past several months chasing down anything and everything.

He's killed vampires and werewolves and ghosts. He didn't know a ghost could die again until he found a way to kill it.

He stands in the arena, knife in one hand, a silver blade just like this whole damned city. He would never have believed such a place existed. It was not what he'd expected.

He expected a lair, and a population of dozens. He expected vampires and maybe werewolves or some other pet, perhaps a demon. He wouldn't mind sticking his knife through a demon's heart.

Nick Hunter now, however, expects to die. The undefeated will not be easily defeated. Every warrior who has set foot in this arena has fallen.

He expected a crowd, but the stands are empty, mostly empty, occupied by the vilest, most blood-thirsty of beasts the dark has ever produced. He recognizes none of them. The stink of death is heavy, the stench of rot and decay, the scent of blood. He's familiar with these things.

The stone door behind him slides shut. It's a heavy door. He cannot break through it. The walls are tall. He cannot climb them. The queen, whoever she is, sits in her throne high above, looking down at him, attended to by her servants and guests and...

His opponent's door does not open. His opponent, this undefeated champion, does not come forward. Is the queen of this underworld so far away that his aim would be inaccurate? She is. He aims anyway, closes one eye and holds his arm as steady as he can. He trembles. It's not a good shot. The bullets, silver though they may be, might be insufficient to destroy whatever she is. He lowers his aim. Looks around him. There are creatures in the stands, vampires and dogs and other things he's only just learned exist. Some of those shadows move or drift. They barely seem interested. A group of beasts drinks. Perhaps it's beer, perhaps it's blood, but they've got mugs full of it and they're not even looking out onto the arena.

From other places in the stands, places swallowed by darkness, other things may watch intently. They'd said he would fight in the spectacle, that it would be a grand occasion, that death itself would attend.

He smells death and wonders why it hasn't come yet for him.

He looks up at the queen again, in the highest of balconies. She looks down on him and maybe she smiles, but she's not alone. She's far away, one of the few in the stands actually watching him. He cannot see her face, not clearly, nor the face of the man beside her, nor the servant standing there.

Is this some sort of test? Is it that there is no creature to fight, no undefeated anything stepping into this arena to face him? Must he climb the walls, put a bullet in the queen's brain, as all of the spectators move to defend her? Must he kill them all?

That was always his intention.

He counts fewer than fifty. Those are not the best odds. Does he start by randomly killing the onlookers? Or is it merely the queen he must worry himself over?

He's not a climber. He's wounded. He's weak. He might not make it. He strides across the field of battle. He senses the weight of all who walked before him. How many made the attempt? How did they die? Starvation? Thirst? Beasts of the night, maybe their deaths had been less than clean and less than civil.

From the center of the field, he can still see the figures in the balcony. There are other balconies, other figures. Some of the creatures in the stands move. Some shift. Some are things other than what they'd appeared. He doesn't know and doesn't care. He'll get to them all, eventually.

He checks his gun. The magazine holds ten rounds. Silver bullets. Best at short range. He has only one spare magazine left. Fewer than fifty creatures, but more than twenty. His aim might be off. He's weak and uneven and therefore shaky. Cannot afford to waste a shot.

The knives are silver too.

In this silver city, he doubts that makes any difference.

7.

Jack Harlow assesses his surroundings, the things in the dark, the height of the balcony, the predisposition of the servant, Eulalia. He was never the fighter, always the watcher, but he's not completely incapable. But what odds face him?

If he's meant to be trapped here, must he fight his way out? If so, can he help Nick escape, too?

He stands.

"Sit," Tania says.

"What do you see in me now?" Jack asks, stepping toward the edge of the balcony. It's a long drop, nearly sheer, to the top of the stands, and a good distance from the front. Even there, it's a long drop into the arena – or a tough climb.

Jack Harlow is a lot of things – and he's not a lot of things, too. He's not stupid. There's no surviving in the arena without assistance, and there's no one to help him if he joins Nick down there. They'll die together, just as they almost did in Orlando months ago. The creatures of the dark might be unable to hurt Jack directly – he questions that – but certainly time has no such restriction. They'll die first of thirst, maybe exposure, maybe the silver dust on the air. They'll die of hunger. Maybe they'll turn on each in their delirium. There's a great many ways in which time can kill two men on a barren field – in a wide hole, a pit, this self-proclaimed arena.

"What I see," Tania says, "is a man who believes he has no friends. Everyone you've ever loved has abandoned you. Your father – the great Jonathan Harlow – not so great, was he? Your lover – your sparrow, I can see her now."

Jack's fists tightened as she spoke.

"I see her dying with you, dying while you helplessly stood over her." Tania offers a sad smile. "So sad, Jack Harlow. You should've loved the vampire instead."

"Who are you, really?" He's a watcher. The names of things come to him, usually, but sometimes those names and descriptions that he knows, knows inherently, are wrong – or incomplete. He's seen it, he's seen it even in himself, and he's seeing it again now. Does his *gift* – *curse* – lie to him?

Tania is a seer. But that's not a thing, is it? That's not a type of creature. That's a skill. Is she human?

"I'm more than you can imagine," Tania says, "but I, yes, primarily human."

"You read thoughts."

"I *read*."

"Thoughts. Emotions. Futures?"

Tania glances at Eulalia. The scarred servant touches Jack's arm and says, "You're becoming tedious."

Jack whirls on her. "Am I?"

Eulalia cowers.

Tania jumps to her feet. "I can have you killed."

"You can't. I'm a watcher, so I'm protected."

"You're not protected from everything."

"But I'm more than that, aren't I?"

Tania lowers her voice. "I will send you to the pit."

"Now," Jack says, "I'm scared."

Tania's eyes narrow and her lip curls.

"Who gives you your orders?" Jack asks. "Who really runs this place? My father?"

Tania laughs.

Eulalia pulls on Jack's arm, tries to draw him away, distract him, hold him back.

"The marketplace was a lie," he says. "This whole

thing, a charade. To ease me into this? To lure me? What for?"

"To trap you, my dear," Tania says. "To hold you. To keep you. You'll be in the arena one day, too, Jack Harlow. One day soon. And you will review your regrets and your bad decisions, and you will die, ranting, slavering, a madman facing the undefeated. And you will beg, beg *me*, for forgiveness. But Silver Blade is not a place of forgiveness. It's a pit. A pit over a pit over a pit."

Jack shakes Eulalia off his arm and grabs Tania by the throat. She smiles. "Ah, so you do have a temper. You've got blood in you, after all. Good. You'll need blood if you're to survive." Jack realizes there are dogs in the balcony now, a half dozen of them, a semi-circle of jaws and drawn blades. He lessens his grip. "You'll have to fight, Jack Harlow. It didn't have to be this way."

The dogs have him now, one on either arm. Jack releases Tania. He glances out at Nick Hunter in the arena. The man is close enough now to this side to recognize him. The shock is visible in his eyes. He aims his gun. Jack smiles. That kind of weapon doesn't have infinite range. From the far side of the arena, a man could hit the wall but probably not a target, not up here. Even from the center of the arena, it might be a tricky shot. But Nick Hunter isn't at the far end of the arena anymore, and he isn't at the center of the arena. He's at the very edge of it. It's still a long shot, and uphill, and Jack's not entirely sure he wouldn't be the target. Jack couldn't hit a target from this distance. But the hunter probably can.

Nick Hunter, at the edge of the arena, pulls the trigger.

8.

The dogs are on Nick the instance he pulled the trigger. They come from everywhere, near and far, a dozen or more. And his aim is true. He drops six of the beasts before they reach him – head shots, all – and wounds three others. By the time they reach him, he's drawn his sword.

Time isn't the enemy, after all. Nick grins as he slashes at the nearest of the dogs.

But they are all armed, and more skilled. Nick isn't a swordsman; he was a hunter, and these dogs aren't his typical prey.

He won't go down without putting on a good show. That's what they paid for, right? That's what they brought him here for, wasn't it?

The rest of the audience, those creatures that aren't the dogs, that aren't the soldiers of the queen, are on the edges of their seats. They lean forward. They watch with all their intensity.

They surround him. But a strange thing: Nick Hunter no longer trembles. He feels no weakness, just adrenaline. It fuels him. Strengthens him. He is no vampire, no supernatural entity, but he is something – a hunter – and he has his own strength and his own fury.

He unleashes it.

He cuts the head clean off the next dog.

The woman, the queen, the damn seer who first saw him in this godforsaken place, calls from her balcony. "Leave the reviled. The undefeated will take him."

The dogs back away. Almost a dozen lay dead in the field.

She leaves. The dogs retreat through small openings in the walls, openings which close immediately behind them. Nick surveys the field. A few of the wounded remain. He feels no need to let them suffer. He looks up at the balcony, at the damned queen, at Jack Harlow, watcher and DarkWalker, at the scarred Eulalia. He'd had a clear shot. How did he miss?

Maybe he hadn't.

The queen turns away. The servant tugs at Jack Harlow. He does not look pleased.

Nick goes about ending the suffering of the snarling beasts. Someone in the audience applauds, a lone, slow clapping that goes on for a while, but the darkness swallows its source.

9.

Two dogs drag Jack Harlow from the balcony. They grimace with the pain of it, they growl in the backs of their throats, but they do it. Jack Harlow's immunity is not complete and all encompassing.

"I should have told you how it works here," Tania says as they walk. She leads the way through a twisting corridor. Eulalia hurries behind them. "Every man, every woman, for themselves. There are levels. Silver Blade is a leveled city, deep in the earth, a former mine but more than that. The deeper you go, the darker it gets, and the more dangerous. The struggle, of course, is to get higher. But this is it, here, the highest you can get. There's no going to the surface, not for us. The surface calls itself Silver Blade, too, but it's a different place, and it's got different rules. *Your father.* He made sure of it."

The corridor twists and descends. The dogs tighten their grip to combat the pain, as though they can take all of it up front and get it over with. Jack struggles against them, but he hasn't got the strength. Yet.

"I scratched and clawed my way to the top," Tania says as they reach their destination, a room with a hole in the center of the floor, a ragged, jagged, rough cut through the rock. The dogs drag Jack to its edge. Fires burn in two braziers on either side of the pit, big red fires in deep iron cauldrons. "If I could see the future, Jack Harlow, I would know if we'll meet again."

The dogs toss him forward. Jack resists. Twists. Shifts his weight. But he goes. He takes one of the dogs with him, but they go down, dropping into the darkness, falling, wrestling even as they fall. The dog bounces off the side of the wall. It sounds like a bone cracks. Then they're in open air, still falling. It's a long fall. A plunge. Jack's eyes don't work in the total darkness, not exactly, so he's not prepared when the fall abruptly ends.

CHAPTER FOUR

1.

The woman with green veins under translucent skin drags Naomi into her lair. No matter how much she tries to slip sideways through time, she cannot slip the cuffs, and her servants – pets – scramble over themselves behind her.

The woman goes on, talking about whatever it is she's saying, in a language Naomi's never heard. The words are old, dusty, guttural, and rough. She says things, and she asks questions, and she tugs Naomi forward by the cuffs. The chains are solid, but possibly silver, which means they're more malleable than iron or steel. She cannot simply snap them open; Naomi is not a creature of brutish strength. But given enough time, she'll be able to twist them enough to escape.

Naomi thought the lair was just a dead end corridor when she first saw it, but it's most certainly a home with definition. There's a corner for shit and piss. There's a corner for the bones that remain of whatever else they've managed to catch and consume. The things on leashes, three of them, are not like the dogs above, but they're not unlike dogs. They're not entirely mindless, but they're not up to mental acrobatics. The woman – Naomi would know more if she could discern the words.

Languages can be tricky things. Some are easy to jump between, like Italian to Spanish, or German to English. Others are far more problematic. Basque, however, was difficult to master, and Mandarin was slippery. Akkadian was not easy. Neither was Arabic. But no matter how skilled a tongue, no one can know all languages, living and dead, and no one can decipher all intentions. There's nothing familiar about the words this woman speaks. They're not merely meaningless sounds, that much is obvious. There's structure, there's repetition, there's resonance and intent behind it. Naomi says nothing. In her experience, it's always been best to pretend at mute ignorance.

The chain does not give Naomi a long reach. The woman drives a silver spike into the rock wall to hold the other end. It will not easily break or budge. Naomi's already working on her end of the chain and the cuffs. She has no desire to be anyone's next meal.

The beasts go to the third corner of the room, where there's something of a nest, gathered clothes and such to sleep on, and they curl up around each other like week-old kittens. The woman examines Naomi. Touches her arm, her shoulder, the side of her face. Asks another question.

Naomi says, in English, "I don't understand."

The woman smiles. Her lips glow faintly green.

"Will you let me go?" Naomi asks, shifting to her first language, Creole, which has always been her most comfortable. She uses her calmest voice and her softest volume. She's not playing at meek so much as projecting serenity. A lack of threat. "I have no anger for you, but I do have friends."

The woman responds. It's dismissive. It's practically vicious. The green in her eyes flares as she speaks. She's shifted to another language, as well. The musicality of it is different.

"I still don't understand."

The woman snarls. She returns to the brazier in the center of the room, where a small fire burns. She speaks to the flames. They dance in response. That's a trick Naomi would love to learn, but she doubts she'll have the time. She listens to the words, and she listens to the language, and she begins to find its rhythms and cadence. She has to start somewhere. She'll probably slip her bonds before she breaks the language.

That's okay. She's less interested in communication than escape.

The fires, in response to the green-veined woman's words, rise in twin pillars, and seem to take on shapes not far from human before collapsing again into the fire. The woman repeats her words. The flames rise again, and collapse as quickly, with a puff of black smoke. The woman curses in her ancient language. Her beasts mewl in response.

Naomi steps forward. The chains allow her that much reach but little more. She looks at the woman, nods once, then looks into the brazier. She sees nothing special, but she recites the words, mimicking the sounds and inflections. Even if she doesn't know what she says, she gets the words right, or close to right. The flames flicker in response. Figures almost take shape, but fail, just as they had for her captor.

Naomi meets the woman's eyes. The woman stares with – it's hard to read the emotions in her eyes and expression. Wonder? Distaste? She doesn't know if this is a good idea, if she's just quickening her own death rather than endearing herself to her captor.

After a moment, Naomi says the words again, and the woman joins her, adding her voice. The fiery bodies rise more strongly – not more than a foot high, either one, but they hold their shape longer. If a consciousness inhabits those flames, it – they – grow more confident. But it's still not enough to give them life, or sentience, or enslave them or whatever it is the green-veined woman intends.

Purposefully, Naomi fumbles a couple of the words, reverses sounds, jumbles the rhythm. She doesn't know what might rise from those flames. She doesn't know she's not meant to be a sacrifice. The binds that hold her won't hold forever. Silver is an extraordinarily weak metal. And while many of the creatures of the dark might fear its poisonous effect on them, it has no such effect on Naomi. Silver doesn't weaken her and doesn't kill her. It doesn't make her subservient or bring on madness or befuddle her senses. Other poisons might. She's a master of poisons. Her pouch contains a number of them. Her pouch holds more than seems possible. It really holds nothing; it's a portal to a place, a place that barely exists, where she stores things, powders and herbs and spices and minerals, and even weapons. She needs nothing from her pouch to get escape these cuffs. She needs only time.

So she starts again. Reciting the words. Getting them wrong. It frustrates the woman, and it frustrates whatever exists inside the fire. The beasts whine in the background, ignored but not forgotten.

2.

Nick Hunter circles the arena. He tests all the doors. They're stone and will not move for him. He attempts to jump and climb, to scale the walls, but they're twice as high as he can reach. He walks around the perimeter and taps the wall with the flat end of his sword.

It's not even really his sword.

He's replaced the magazine in his Oliveri .357. He's got his own knives. They never tried to disarm him here. Arrogant bastards. He looks up at the ceiling, beyond the reach of the scattered fires. It's just a sea of darkness above him. It could be the actual night sky, but for the lack of stars, moons, suns, and clouds. So it's more rock. Dirt. Metal. He'll bring the whole thing crashing down on Silver Blade. He'll bury this city.

The fires that light the arena die slowly, but they are dying. The light grows dim. Shadows in the stands follow his every movement. One person out there – one creature, one beast, one something that watches from the murk, claps every so often, responding when Nick tries another door, when Nick reaches for the top of the wall. He has pinpointed the source of this, a spot so dark it might be an abyss, a place unreached by any firelight. You, he says, if only to himself, I'll take your hands before I take your head.

The dogs he'd killed have plenty of blades, all silver, but no additional firepower. They're not powerful things, just mindless brutes. They're not better armed because they are expected to die.

They'd caught Nick in the streets of Richmond. He'd been following the trail of a particular vampire. Not one of those mindless beasts he had spent so much time destroying before. This lived in an apartment, a converted bottling plant, and drove a car – only at night, of course. It lived as a normal man, entertained guests on a rooftop patio, and prowled downtown, under the CSX rail tracks near the James River. Nick had interrupted it in an alley off Dock Street. He'd wounded it. It fled, presumably to its warehouse home with his comfortable carpeting and high definition television and granite countertops. *They* came out of a white moving truck, a dozen dogs. They bound him, hooded him, drove him some distance, brought him under the earth, presented him as a great hero to their queen.

When I get out of here, Nick Hunter thinks, I'll go back to Richmond and finish what I started.

Nick Hunter doesn't believe in death. Not his own. He doesn't accept that he can be defeated. He will not succumb to the undefeated, not in this arena or any other. He will triumph. He knows this, because in all the world there's only one person he's ever considered an ally who isn't dead. And that person – Jack Harlow – is here, under the earth with him, beside the very same queen who had promised Nick a great hunt. "Then why drag me here against my will?" She had only smiled.

He wonders if everyone and everything in this shallow city is here unwillingly.

Nick makes his way to the center of the arena. Pacing won't do him any good. He sits cross-legged in the very center of the arena, on the dusty rock, facing away from the dog corpses and away from the balcony. There are other balconies, not so high, and some of these are occupied. He looks at each. He cannot tell what they are, if any of those are vampires, but that doesn't matter. Vampires are his specialty. His area of expertise. But other creatures prowl the dark, and he's perfectly capable of killing those, as well.

He lays his sword on the ground in front of him, sets his hands, palm up, on his knees, and closes his eyes. Deep breaths. Focus. Concentrate. This is a big arena with many ways out. How can he reach one? Will his audience, limited as it may be, allow him to escape? Will they declare him victor over the undefeated?

He doesn't do this for glory. Now, it's for his life, and to continue his mission. He remembers the first time he saw Jack Harlow. The watcher had tried to defend his lover from an *imp*. Nick hadn't even known such a thing existed. Jack had fought for love then. What brings him to Silver Blade?

The answer is obvious. *He* brought Jack to Silver Blade. They couldn't touch him, not in the same way, so they tricked him, promised that his friend, his one friend in the world, was trapped here and needing rescuing.

It takes a lot of effort to not curl his hands into fists.

As a reward for his restraint, his fan in the stands claps again.

Nick Hunter turns his head. He cannot see with his eyes closed. Nor can he see through the thick dark. Is someone in those stands cheering his little defeats, offering encouragement in some difficult-to-understand way, or trying to send some sort of message? If it's Morse code, it's lost on the hunter. He never learned it, never needed it. If it's some other form of language, he wouldn't even know. If it's a version of hot and cold – is the clapping supposed to indicate that he's doing something right?

Of course he's reading too much into it. There's no meaning whatsoever. How right can it be to sit in the middle of this arena of the undefeated?

He turns his head one way, then the other, but the tempo of the clapping remains steady both in tempo and volume. He takes a deep breath. The world smells like silver now. The dogs must be inured to it. If they were true werewolves, wouldn't they succumb? Isn't silver some sort of poison, for wolves and vampires alike? Why build a city, a *society*, in an abandoned silver mine? Because the shallow city existed before the mine. And it's purpose wasn't to be a sanctuary, but to be a prison.

Someone or something has sentences Jack Harlow to life in prison. Nick was taken merely as bait.

He takes another deep breath, attempts to keep his fists steady and open. There's nothing to be gained by punching rock or stone or metal. There's nothing to be gained by lashing out against the unseen and the unreachable. Time – the undefeated – drifts around him, ebbs and flows. Is time as malleable as silver in this shallow city?

How does that help him?

Another deep breath, and Nick opens his eyes. He peers into the darkness, into the stands, marking each individual creature out there. More than ten. His bullets might be useless anyhow. The sword with the silver blade sits in front of him. Silver is weak. It's not the best choice for a weapon like that. It's already warped and dinged and twisted, though it still seems straight. The hilt is not silver. The grip and guard are steel. The pommel is silver, and once held a gem of some sort, something big, undoubtedly shiny, something that made the sword special, if not magical. Nick doesn't have to believe in magic to believe someone might else have. It's not a fancy blade, but this hilt hadn't been meant for it.

Nick runs his finger along the edge of the blade. It's sharp enough, but dulled by every use. There are not engravings, no hidden symbols, no clues, but there's something in the sword – inside the blade – something he can use.

There's movement in the stands. He ignores it. Nick picks up the sword and strides toward the stone door through which he had entered the arena. He feels stronger now, as though well rested and well fed, though he's neither of these things. What he is, though, is determined.

He doesn't even look back to see if the queen has returned to her balcony to watch him. There's no sport in this arena. It's just one of many prisons within the prison of Silver Blade.

The stone is a door, a door locked from the outside. Nick tries to push it, tries to pull it, but the stone resists all movement. But when the dogs opened it for him, it had slid easily aside. The weight of it had been perfectly balanced to function. Only the lock restricts it.

Nick swings the sword at the stone. It clatters. The cutting edge of the sword cracks the stone. There's no question which will outlast the other. Nick swings again. And again. The sound of sword against stone makes a kind of music. His appreciative audience keeps the rhythm with that lone and lonely semblance of applause.

Ah, but the rhythm has increased. A game of hot and cold after all.

The edge of the sword twists. Nick doesn't stop. Chips of stone fall away from the door. Little chips. Nothing substantial. Stone chips and stone dust versus the finest silver blade ever constructed. The blade bends. The edge of the blade breaks off. The piece of silver flies past Nick's face, nearly taking his eye.

He pauses.

But only for a moment. Nick swings again and again, no longer overhead but side to side, swiping and slashing, the reverberations of every strike resonating in his hand and in his heart. He gives it a war cry, screaming at the wall and the door and the arena, screaming at the sword and the queen who gave it to him.

Did she even know?

Does Nick?

He hacks at the stone door like it might make any difference. The sword fractures. The sword shatters. Nick stops screaming, stops slashing. But his audience, the one creature out there, is on its feet and applauding like a madman. "Bravo!" the creature cries with a voice neither male nor female, a voice barely even human. "Bravo!"

Breathless, Nick steps back from the stone and settles on one knee. He still holds the steel hilt of the sword. The cross-guard. The pommel without its prize. The grip, which extends four inches beyond the guard, a thin and notched piece of steel hidden within the silver blade. A key.

Nick Hunter thrusts the key into the slot within the door, the keyhole, the barely noticeable and never-before-utilized keyhole. He twists. The stone door slides aside easily.

The reviled exits the floor of the arena.

3.

The flame figures rise and fall as Naomi repeats the words with her captor. They struggle to break free of whatever binds them, and Naomi's sure that even conflating the words she's aiding them. She breathes a few words between sets while the woman with the translucent skin and electric green veins breathes.

Naomi doesn't need that much breath.

Quietly, while chanting old and unknowable words, she's slipped one wrist free of the cuffs. Without looking, barely moving, she pulls something from her pouch. Something dangerous.

In the midst of another series of words, she falters, and stumbles to one knee. The woman snarls and hisses, and grabs Naomi, pulls her to her feet. Naomi clings to her, just for a moment, her hands close together as though still bound by silver. "Thank you," she whispers, words the woman cannot understand, soft and gentle so that the tone is obvious. She releases other words, too, mimicking the tone, even as her poisons seep through translucent skin.

Naomi has worked with many powders and potions. This seeps into the woman's skin and into her bloodstream, where the green turns violently red. Crimson blood spreads quickly, visibly, from the woman's shoulder to her head and heart, to the extremities of her limbs.

Her beasts whimper and growl and rise, hackles up, teeth bared. They leap at Naomi.

She slips sideways through time. An old trick, but a useful one. She only gets to the other side of them.

The woman lets loose a string of obscenities in her ancient language. The figures in the fire burst forward.

They're small and weak, but they're flames, two of them. She slashes her arms to let her crimson-tainted blood spill freely. The fire sprites, whatever they are, soak up what's left of the green. They spit out the poisons. They turn toward Naomi.

She runs. She slips sideways through time, she sprints, she dodges this way and that. She's quickly beyond the reach of the woman's pets, but the sprites are unrestricted.

Naomi bangs into timbers supporting the ceiling. She stumbles into walls like a pinball. The dark is too dense, the corridors not as straight as they had seemed, not as straight as they should be. This mine suffers from lousy design.

Naomi runs straight into a beast, a big, muscled thing with silver teeth that sparkle in the glow of the fire sprites. It roars, and swipes at her with talons that gouge the wall.

The fire sprites leap upon her. They burn where they land on her back. They screech in a fiery language. Her clothes catch the flames. She stumbles. She rolls across the unforgiving floor of the mine. She rolls over tracks for mining carts. She rolls out of the way of talons as that other beast lashes out again.

Darkness swallows her as the fire sprites lose their power. The beast, though, does not. It grabs Naomi, piercing her shoulder with one of those talons, and it roars with all its hot, rancid breath.

On the verge of losing consciousness, Naomi swings her one good arm – below the pierced shoulder, nothing responds – striking the creature's teeth with the silver cuff and tearing open her hand. It howls again.

"I'll haunt your gut," she says through gritted teeth. Overwhelmed with pain, she's not sure she's actually said the words. She blinks and loses an entire second, maybe two. She blinks again and loses three. She tries to block out the pain, but the creature has her in its talons and every movement sends fresh waves of agony through every centimeter of her nervous system. She screams something at it, something incoherent, but the creature is merely a creature, and it means to devour her.

She kicks at it. The movement tears at her shoulder. She does more damage to herself than to the beast. It shoves her against the rock wall.

The fire sprites flash brightly. She'd thought they were gone. Maybe it's only a trick of vision, a trick of the pain. The talons release her. She's flung to the side. She's bleeding badly, her left arm won't work at all, she can't feel it through the pain, doesn't know if it's still there or hanging by threads of muscle and sinew. She sees the green blood, bright iridescent green, under the skin of the woman. All the crimson, all the poison, has been purged.

Naomi hovers on the edge of consciousness. She fights against it, but the pain is too much, and she's lost too much blood. She tries to slip sideways through time, but merely collapses. Crashing into the ground, she blinks again and loses three seconds. There's a reprieve in the darkness of oblivion. A coldness. She tries again, one last time, a slip sideways through time, back the way she came, away from this creature and the fire sprites and the woman with her ancient words.

But she doesn't know the way she came.

She doesn't know where she is or why. Silver Blade? What the hell is that? A mine? Really? A city of the undead and dangerous? A trap? Is there safety on the surface?

The creature with the talons howls. It's got the woman's neon green blood in its mouth – but the blood is corrosive, like acid, burning away at the creature's flesh, maybe burning away at Naomi's.

She feels the icy breath of death on the nape of her neck, in her veins under the burning, at the edges of consciousness. She closes her eyes, welcoming the soothing darkness, but resisting even to her last breath. She pushes forward, outward, away from where she is, a sideways step through time with all her power, random and final. And even then, she refuses to stop breathing.

CHAPTER FIVE

.

1.

The Scavenger sees in the dark. She sees the light first, the smallest shred of it managing to make its way down the shaft. It's a low, weak light. It shines on nothing. But it signals a fall. There's always someone or something ready to be thrown to the pits.

She scurries closer to the edge of the water and watches not one but two creatures dropping – one of the dogs, so whatever they threw must've been strong enough to not go alone. She trills. It's a small pleasure, but there's little enough to be had.

She pushes her canoe out. It wasn't always her canoe. Whoever made it is long dead, or they'd be able to repair the holes, stop the leaks. One day, she'll set off onto the water and she'll sink, and what then? No death is easy, especially not the death under the lake. She pushes out and rows to where the dog and the – man? – crash into the lake.

Usually, the surface is still, like a mirror, though there's nothing to reflect. Little animals drift along the surface sometimes, insects and the like, but nothing goes deep. Around its edges, the scavenger's not the only one who saw the falling prize.

Often, they survive the fall. They don't always survive the water.

The scavenger rows out toward the center, where both newcomers struggle with the water and against each other. Blood on the water. She'll have to be quick. There won't be time to take both. That's disappointing. The human might be interesting, might have knowledge, might have skills. But the dog will have silver. Any blade is better than none, and there are few of those around here. She keeps her claws sharp, but she's getting older and she's slowing down. Death awaits. A blade extends her reach and might extend her nights. She'll take it. She'll take it, and row back to shore, and she'll probably watch the human succumb to the terrors of the depths.

She doesn't know how deep the lake goes. It's bottomless, essentially, because of the tentacles at the bottom, the tendrils, the teeth.

Someone else on the surface, another canoe, another racing toward the prize, but she's strong and swift and she'll tear its eyes out. Even in the dark, even in total darkness, even when the pitch is thick and layered, you need eyes to survive.

Maybe not under the lake. She doesn't know if there are eyes beneath the surface.

She gets to them first. The struggle has stopped. The dog is dead. The human has the blade. She's surprised, but she doesn't let it slow her down. "Careful," she says, helping him climb onto the canoe. It rocks. He's not a water creature. He's not used to floating. He'll tip the canoe if he's stupid, and they'll both die. *"Careful!"* she snaps. She takes the blade and puts it behind her in the canoe. She holds the human by the back. The glares at the other canoe, the other scavenger glaring back. She bares her teeth and hisses. But the other scavenger isn't an idiot. He knows there's two things that fell, and two of them. They can take one each and rob the depths of their prize.

So there's no fight. She rows away, back toward her shore, leaves the dead dog for her competition. She's happy with its blade. She's happy with the human. It hurt to touch him, it burned, so he's not just a human. He's a real prize. She resists an urge to cast him back to the waters, leave him to the tentacles. He breathes loud.

He's gasping, of course, that's to be expected. But he's loud and noisy, he's not accustomed to the waters, he doesn't know what waits beneath the surface. She'll have to tie him, if she means to profit any. She's already got the silver, but she didn't just take the blade. The human is weak and winded and can't know what's happened. He's been tossed into the pit, discarded, sacrificed, devoured by darkness. He'll have a story to tell, at the very least, and scavengers like a good story now and then. To pass the night. To keep warm in the darkness.

He's not just loud, he's heavy, but not as heavy as a dog so she made the better choice. More meat on the dog, but she's not starved. More potential here. More mystery. She likes to discover things. Her hidey hole, like all the others, is a cove off the lake – cove being a big word for a small place. The human splashes as he crawls from the canoe to the shore, that can't be helped, but still she says, "Quiet." She pushes the canoe enough out of the water that it won't float away. She looks back. The other scavenger is dragging his prize back to his undersized cove. She hisses. She would have had both, but for the blood. There's movement under the surface, she can see it. It's a kind of frenzy. They're awake down there, awake and agitated. She spits at the lake. Let them prowl. Let them swim. One day, if she's lucky, she'll claim something from the depths as her prize, and that night she'll dine well.

The human says something. She doesn't listen. He's still too loud. She slaps him once in the mouth. "*Quiet*," she says, her voice never more than a whisper. There are only whispers on the lake. There are only whispers in the dark. Anything else attracts attention. More than scavengers prowl these shores.

It's a big lake. She keeps quiet, keeps to herself, keeps her prizes. She's the swiftest and strongest and smartest and slyest of the scavengers – but only of the scavengers.

She's got a hole to sleep in. She pushes the human toward it. He complies. He remains quiet. He sloshes, but he's not the noisiest thing she's recovered off the surface. The cave meanders a little. It's a twisting, turning decline, but it's not far before they reach her den. Her home. With her hearth and her fire, her cloths, her prizes.

"You make too much noise," she tells it.

"I didn't mean to," he says. His voice is at a respectable level, though still louder than she'd prefer. He's a good one, she decides, a quick learner, without much struggle in him but something. "Where am I?"

"They threw you in the pit, they did," she says. She snatches a piece of old bread, hard, crusty inside and out, and shoves it at him. "You fell."

"Where am I?"

Maybe he's not so smart as she thought. "Inside the pit."

"And you?" he asks. "Who are you? Not merely a scavenger."

"Scavenger."

"Do you have a name?"

"Of course I have a name," she says. But she doesn't, not really. No need for names and titles in the dark.

"I'm Jack Harlow," he says.

"That's a lot of name."

"Call me Jack."

"*Jack*." She likes the way she can spit the name out, quick and easy, nothing complicated like some of those other names and titles she's heard. Lord of this, Regent of that, Overseer of the Underneath, Lord High

Almighty, Watcher of the Dark. Too many mouthfuls. If you need a breath in the middle of your name, it's too much name.

"And you are?"

"Doesn't matter," she says. "I salvaged you off the surface. You're mine, you and all you possess. I want your silver, I want your steel, I want your iron, I want your gold. I want your stories, too, *Jack*, and I may want your flesh. Ain't starving here, no, but there ain't enough to share."

"This bread," Jack says, chewing, "is good."

It's a lie. A polite lie. She knows it, he knows it. There ain't nothing good about the bread. She stole it. She found it and took it. She eats it because it eases her hunger, and no one seems to notice or care. She says, "I can get more."

"Where is it from?"

"Secret."

"I don't plan to stay here."

"There's nowhere else," she says.

He points back the way they'd come. "I came down. I'll go up."

"There is no up."

"There must be."

"Then it's a secret," the scavenger says, "and a secret that ain't mine to share."

He moves. "I can't stay here."

She's on him in an instant, claws extended so he'll feel them. He burns. She doesn't want to touch him. "Not yet."

"Am I a prisoner?"

She laughs. "You're my *prize*. I salvaged you. I could've left you to die. The waters are *hungry*." She starts going through his pockets, searching for pockets, scrambling over him because there must be metals. "You and yours are mine. I risked my *life*."

He swats at her hands, so she scratches him. Not too deep, but to send a message. "*Stop*," she says. "When I've taken what I want, I'll let you go."

"Will you?"

She hisses and jumps away from him, toward the mouth of her den. She hisses again. "What are you? Why do you hurt?"

"I'm poison," he says. It's a lie, but not entirely.

"You're a *watcher*." She grins. "You made the shallow city."

"I did not."

"You, your kind, whatever." She grins again. "Oh, you must have stories. Tell me a story. Tell me."

"A story?"

"A good one," she says. "With adventure and romance and *mystery*."

He blinks. He's confused. He knows nothing. He's stupid, is what he is. She adds, "The dark is made up of stories."

"I didn't know that."

"You live in the dark, you learn," she says. "There's claws and teeth, and there's stories. To survive the night."

"You mean like fairy tales? Little Red Riding Hood? Hansel and Gretel?"

"Those stores, I know," she says. "Something new. Something you did."

"I haven't done anything."

"Something you saw."

He sighs. It's a pathetic sound. She hopes he doesn't make it often. "I've seen a lot."

"Tell me about one."

"I saw an *acheri* once."

She's never heard of it. "A what?"

"A kind of ghost," he says. "A kind of spirit, actually."

The scavenger settles down to listen, though she keeps herself between the human and the mouth of her den.

"It was terrible, actually," Jack says. "I saw her climbing a fire escape."

She crinkles her nose. She doesn't know what a fire escape is, either.

"Iron steps leading to a window," Jack says. "So there's a back entrance to a building in case of fire."

"Have you ever escaped a fire on one of these?"

"I haven't, no," he says. "You want this story or no?"

"Please."

"I saw her climbing the fire escape," Jack says. "Three, four stories up, I'm not sure. She scratched at the window, then stepped through the glass."

"She shattered it?"

"No. She's a kind of spirit, remember."

"Only a spirit, then, got it."

"She crawled through the window because inside, she found a child, three or four years old."

The scavenger hisses. Meat that young hasn't had time to marbleize properly. She has her preferences. When there's a choice, she'll take them ripe, neither overdone nor under.

"The acheri, it wants to devour children."

"Why?"

"Revenge."

"What did this child do to it?"

"Nothing."

"Your *acheri*," she says, the word slimy on her tongue, "doesn't understand revenge."

"Maybe not. But this night, there was someone else there already, a hunter, waiting in the dark for just such a thing. See, there'd been several dead children already, and someone in the neighborhood, this one person, he was wise enough to know what it was."

"So the child didn't die?"

"The child didn't die."

"And the hunter?"

"He caught his prey. The acheri."

"What did he do with it?" Then she cocked her head. "How did he catch a spirit that sneaks through glass?"

"With red gold."

"You got any red gold?"

Jack shakes his head. "No, I don't."

"You're not a good storyteller."

"No, I suppose not."

"What did he do with the acheri?"

"He cast it back."

"How?"

"I don't know, exactly," Jack says. "Secrets that aren't mine."

She grins. "If the acheri was cast back into a pit, a pit like this one, she might be here in the dark with us now."

"I doubt that."

"She might still be hungry."

"This was far away," Jack says. "A thousand miles. Boston."

"I've heard of Boston."

"And you know it's nowhere near here."

She shakes her head. "But all the dark is connected, and all the tunnels lead to other tunnels, and all the cities share the same roots."

"Have you been to any other cities?" Jack asks.

"Which one is this?"

"Silver Blade."

"I know that place," she says. "I am of Silver Blade, yes. Born here. Will die here. I scavenge the lake and steal prizes from the mouths under the surface." She shakes her head. "I know no other place. I've always been here."

"Do you know how to reach the surface?"

"The waters are deep and the deep has teeth."

"Have you seen the sky?"

She says nothing. He's not good with stories. He's more questions. She should've taken the dead dog. She did, however, acquire some silver, so that's good. Sharp and useful.

"Have you seen the stars?" he asks.

"I heard a story about the stars," she says. "That when the stars are hungry, they grow big, and they brighten the sky, and they devour tigers and dragons whole."

"I've never heard that story."

"It's just a story," she says. "Just like the stars."

"But I," Jack says, tapping his chest. "I have seen the stars."

"I've seen stars," she tells him, "but never a sky, I don't think. I'd know, wouldn't I? Don't know what a sky looks like, but I've heard of it, I've heard stories, and I have seen stars, but I don't think they're what you think."

"Take me there," Jack says, leaning forward and grabbing both her paws as though they're mated. "Take me to these stars."

She pulls away and shakes her head. "You'll want me dead, you will, if I show you the stars."

He shakes his head. "No. I only want to find my friends."

"*Friends?*" she asks. She spits. "I had a friend once. He tried to eat me."

"Will you help me?"

"Will you give me metal?"

He hesitates. He says, "I don't have any with me, but above the mine, in Silver Blade, I have *metal*."

"Silver?"

"I don't know," he says. "I just know it's metal."

"Silver," she says. "Copper. Iron. Steel."

"And gold, yes, I got that."

She shakes her head, but then she grins. "I'll show you the stars. They are shiny and bright and overhead."

The human moves to get up, but she holds out a paw and narrows her eyes. "If you run," she says, "I'll let you. Run all you want. The dark was eat you. The dark has teeth. You, in the dark, you will die."

"That's always a risk," Jack says. "But I won't run."

"I don't ask for no promise," she tells him. "But on the way, I want more stories. Better stories. That acheri story was awful."

2.

Nick Hunter rounds another corner.

The place is a maze of mine shafts supported by timbers. Sconces every twenty or forty feet light the paths. Twin metal lines in the floor indicate where a cart would have been pushed.

Even with the arena behind him, he feels the undefeated breathing down his neck – as if an invisible, all-powerful creature follows him through the dark. When he was brought to the arena floor, the dogs had dragged him, a half dozen of them. They'd starved him for days, denied him water, everything. His second wind, if he could call it that, won't fuel him for long. He needs water. He needs food. He needs to get out of this hole and close it.

At another intersection, he accepts that he has no idea where he was going. The corridors are all the same, roughly hewn rock, thick wood trunks holding the whole thing together. Random intersections.

Nick follows the tracks. Presumably, they lead to the mine entrance, upwards and outside. He could use a taste of fresh air. The animal reek of the mines have ruined his senses.

Finally, up ahead, there's an elevator, an ancient contraption put together more by sheer intention than engineering prowess. The machinery, all rusting and rickety, is in motion, and four dogs guard it.

Nick charges in swinging. The knife is a good knife. It's his. He slashes through the neck of the first dog before they even know he's there. He plunges it into the chest of the second. They'd all had their weapons out. They all knew he was coming. But he's the hunter, silent, stealthy, as vicious as any of them and better trained.

The elevator cage descends. The shaft is a black hole. It descends and ascends. It doesn't go all the way to the surface, but its highest level does lead out.

It moves slowly.

Whatever's coming, it'll be more challenging than the dogs. The four of them are dead now, scattered, bleeding and twitching and gurgling. They never made a sound, never really put up a struggle. The dogs aren't even dogs. Generations of inbreeding has weakened them. They aren't eternal, not even particularly long-lived. What they are is plentiful.

Nick Hunter searches them for additional guns and ammunition, anything more formidable. He doesn't know what's coming, he doesn't know what waits above, he doesn't know how many levels he'll have to climb. They'll know he's coming.

The cage continues its descent. Whatever's in there, he could trap it, he could do something to affect the machinery. But he'll only be trapping himself underground. He has no wish to die down here.

When the cage comes into sight, there's a man in it, a man easily the size of two, in a custom-made suit, tie and silver tie pin, cuffs, a pocket square. He's scraggily, unshaven and wild haired, and smiling broadly. With a pull of the lever, he stops the cage. "Hunter," he says, opening the cage and stepping out. He barely spares a glance for the fallen dogs. "The seer would like to speak with you."

Nick raises his gun arm. "I'd like to put a stake through her heart."

The big man smiles. "She's not a vampire."

"Just for the pleasure, then." Nick pulls the trigger.

The man, however, is faster than his trigger finger, and bigger. He lunges forward and aside. The bullet strikes the rock wall behind the elevator. The man, with his big, big hand, plucks the gun right out of his hand. Nick responds with the knife, low, straight at the man's gut. Buries the blade inside him. It makes no difference.

With the back of his fist, the man knocks Nick into the wall. Blood spurts from his nose. His lips swell. His eye probably blackens. His brain rattles a bit inside his skull.

"This suit was custom made," the man says, pulling the knife out of his gut and tossing it – and the gun – down the elevator shaft. He comes forward, grabs Nick by the back of his neck and lifts him off the floor. "As I said, the seer wishes to see you." He throws Nick into the elevator cage, follows him in, and pulls shut the door. He starts the cage rising, then removes his suit jacket. It's got an extra flap. There's blood, from the wound, and red blooms on the white shirt beneath. He folds the jacket and carries it in a fist, and doesn't even spare a glance for Nick Hunter.

3.

When Naomi dreams, they're nightmares of the most vicious type. They're not her fears, they're not about anything unknown. They're memories. Her childhood. Her brother. Her family. The streets of Cité Soleil. Tin houses, hurricanes, gunplay, and gangs. They're the nastiest kind of dreams because they're the truest. So she stopped dreaming long ago. She forced them to stop. She used special tinctures and mystical words, yet still, sometimes, especially when she's weak or wounded, the nightmares sneak back into her skull.

She opens her eyes in darkness and knows this is no dream. There were colors in the worst parts of Haiti. There were colors in the worst parts of Miami. Her whole life has been colorful, even if she walks through the night. Darkness, alone, is comfortable, cool, silent, and no threat to Naomi.

This is not the darkness alone. She's on her back. She cannot feel her arm. She feels nothing, in fact, though there should be pain. She tries to move, but no muscles respond except her eyes. She's opened her eyes, and she can look around, but all she sees is the rock ceiling above her, the wood strut struggling to hold open this hole in the earth. She sees its weak points. It's *all* weak points.

Then the translucent woman with the green veins stands over her. Naomi's on something, or the woman is kneeling, neither of which makes sense. The woman smiles with too many teeth. The flickering firelight distorts everything, or Naomi's senses do. She tries to speak but her mouth and tongue are immobile. The woman says something in her old language. She pricks the edge of her own finger with a fingernail. A drop of blue blood forms there. She smears this on Naomi's lips, and Naomi feels it.

Her lips return to her, her lips and mouth and tongue. She asks, "What have you done?" She knows she should be dead. She cannot really move her head, but she can see more than she saw. Her arms are around her. They're not numb. She knows what numb feels like. They're just not there. The woman continues to speak, softly, almost caringly, but her words remain obscure.

The woman moves away. Naomi hears the dogs. She can wriggle her ear. That's got to mean something. She draws a deep breath. Whispers a prayer. She should be dead, but she's not, she's been spared and even saved. The woman returns, leans close, sniffs with a nose that's almost human, and looks directly into Naomi's eyes.

She can move her eyes but she doesn't look away. The woman's eyes glow blue, like that one drop of blood. They're deep eyes, endless and infinite, but they reveal nothing. The woman asks a question.

"I don't feel better," Naomi says. "I feel nothing."

The woman responds.

The tone is suggestive, but the words are as meaningless as scratches on a record. The woman touches Naomi's lip again, another blue drop of blood. She pushes Naomi's mouth open and releases a drop to slide down Naomi's throat. It's cold, much colder than blood should be, and this exchange frightens Naomi. There are a number of creatures who drink or revel in blood, but only a few who give it freely. Usually, such an exchange is not beneficial to the recipient. Naomi tries to resist, but it's already too late. Another drop slides down her tongue and into her esophagus. Under other circumstances, she has enough control over her body to stop and even purge infectious agents. But she's been paralyzed, and her mind almost dissembled from her physicality.

She feels warmth in her chest. Her heart. She hears it beat once. Another drop of blood rolls down her throat. She feels the nails on her fingers and toes. She extends them. She can't see the result, but everything feels right, and there's not the slightest bit of pain. Another drop of blood, however, changes nothing. Her senses don't respond, external or internal senses.

The woman smiles and touches Naomi's forehead – she feels the warmth of her hand – and says something. One of her beasts responds with a questioning yip. Naomi can almost understand the question. The woman responds to the animal, then looks into Naomi's eyes again and says something, a single word, a command.

"I can't rest," Naomi says. "I can't do anything."

But the next drop of blood is pink, and as it slides down Naomi's throat her senses blur and her consciousness drifts. She doesn't see Cité Soleil and she doesn't see her brother. She doesn't see anything at all but oblivion.

4.

The big man drags Nick Hunter into the chamber again. It's a big empty place, though there are the remnants of a tent city being torn down, dogs busy removing wooden posts and cloths and thin temporary walls. At the far end of it: the queen's hole. The seer, as the man says. He drags Nick straight to the cavern and its warren of tunnels behind it. The women in the front area stare at him openly and hungrily. He doesn't know what they are, but he's sure their best futures involves wooden stakes and severed heads.

The seer sits upon her throne surrounded by tapestries and an excessive number of wood columns. She expects they'll protect this chamber from the inevitable cave-in. More women lounge on couches and beds and drink wine – possibly wine. Three silver statuettes, a dancer, a raven, and a tiger, stand exactly where he remembers them.

The scarred woman, Eulalia, curtseys and says, "The lady Tania will see you now."

No response is expected, and Nick gives none. The man holds him in place.

Tania's eyes glisten and her smile twinkles. She presents a point of brightness in the dark. "I want to thank you," she says. "You have played your role excellently."

"My role?"

Tania shakes her head, a remonstration of sorts. "But I don't like you, and I can't release you back into the wild. You're a dangerous man, Nick Hunter, and I fear you'll come back somehow. We drew in the son of Johnathan Harlow, and now he's gone from the shallow city, dropped into the pits, where he will live or die of his own accord. That was the judgement, and the sentence has been carried out."

"Whose judgement?"

"I could have kept him here and played with him," Tania says, ignoring the question. "I could keep you here, but I don't think you'll be any fun." She gives him an exaggerated frown. "I fear you're too violent for my tastes. But fortunately, there is a solution."

"Whose judgement?" Nick asks again. The hand around the back of his neck tightens.

"I've given this some thought," Tania says, rising. "You're a hunter. Specifically a vampire hunter. So I thought the best thing to do is give you one. A vampire, that is. Oh, you'll still be reviled, more than ever before, and you'll go back to the arena. Ultimately, the undefeated will still claim you. You cannot avoid your fate."

A woman steps into the cavern from one of the side caves. She's short but voluptuous, and she's dressed in layers of veils. She's smiling, and Nick knows, on sight, what she is.

"Lady Chandra, meet the vampire hunter, Nick Hunter." Tania smiles. "Nick Hunter, meet the Lady Chandra. I'd like to say that long ago, she lived in a city now consigned to myth, but the truth is she's not much older than you are. I can't say where she's from, or how she was transformed, but you'll have plenty of time to get to know each other."

Before Nick can even resist, the big man pushes him forward, toward the vampire.

"Take extra special care of him, Lady Chandra," Tania says.

Lady Chandra nods briefly but does not smile, then takes Nick from the big man. Her grip is even stronger.

She pulls him close, sniffs his neck, and sinks her teeth. She drinks. It's not at all how Nick expects, and not at all how he remembers. The creatures he's fought have always been nasty, wicked, and cruel. She's tender and even delicate. As his strength dissipates, she stops, and she sweeps him into her arms.

Tania steps closer. She smiles at Nick. "I'm giving you what you most deserve, Hunter." Then she looks at Lady Chandra and commands, "Take them to the pit."

5.

The pit is just that: a hole in the ground. A half dozen dogs and the bear accompany them to the room with the hole. The Lady Chandra hops down, taking Nick Hunter with her.

There are no doors or windows from the room. It's just a pit, ten by ten and twenty feet deep. The vampire lands and bends at the knees like a cat. Some light reaches them from the room above. If any guard remains behind, Nick can't see them from the floor of the hole.

The walls are rock, but not solid. It looks like they might crumble on them if he breathes wrong. It's virtually a sheer climb, and well beyond Nick's ability to scale. Not without tools. Not without help.

The Lady Chandra releases him and smiles. They circle around each other. "I've heard of you," she says.

"I've never heard of you."

"That's a relief, actually." She's smiling. She's not dressed for the mines. In fact, she's as clean as any of the queen's attendants – the menu of her self-proclaimed brothel.

"Why do you listen to her?" Nick asks. "You're obviously stronger."

"I'm not."

"You're a vampire. She's – nothing."

"Oh, she's something, alright," Lady Chandra says. "She controls who goes to the surface and who goes below."

"This is below."

She laughs. "This is just a pit."

Nick's weak, hungry and thirsty, but he knows what the vampire intends to do to him. He won't have it.

They took all his weapons. They took the key he'd used to escape the arena. He had won. He'd escaped the undefeated. This doesn't seem like a fair reward. "How long have you been here?"

"All my vampiric life."

The proximity of her is intoxicating. Like Jia Li, the watcher's vampire friend and lover, Lady Chandra is seductive. Her pheromones are more powerful than any perfume. Her beauty is enhanced by unnatural glamour. She's stunningly beautiful. Her skin looks as soft as silk. Her eyes are hypnotizing. Her lips look delicious.

"What are you waiting for?" Nick asks.

"I thought maybe you'd try something. Defend yourself. Escape." She glances up. "It seems unlikely, but I only know you're the hunter. I don't know what you can do."

"I can kill vampires."

She grins. "Not just by looking at them, apparently."

He lunges forward, feigns one way, throws a punch. It feels useless. His heart's not in it. He knows he's been beaten. She avoids the punch, catches his arm, turns him around, pulls him tight next to her. Her mouth is at his neck. She says, "I can feel your pulse."

He struggles, but it's like struggling against a concrete wall. She's unyielding. She's warm. She's comfortable. She scratches his neck with her teeth and licks the little bit of blood that comes up. "Do you know how transformation works?" she asks. "How a vampire is made?"

"Your *victims*," he says, "rise again."

"No, no, no." She whispers in his ear. "When our meals rise – they're mindless, they're misshapen, they're *mistakes*, and they don't survive long. The world can be so cruel. And there are *hunters.*" She pushes him away. "No, a proper transformation must be intended. Must be careful. A transfer of blood is required, hunter. Not merely a wound. It's a delicate process, and it can take hours. Days."

"And if I'm not willing?"

"Compliance," she says, "will come." She lunges, grabs Nick by the throat, lifts him off his feet, looks up at him with hungry, iridescent eyes, and licks her lips. She squeezes the breath out of him. He kicks, catching her in the stomach, hitting hard enough to steal her breath a moment. She drops him and steps back. "And now I know what it means to be a hunter."

"What's that?"

"A soul full of hatred," she says. "Repulsion. Something happened to make you this way, and now you think you can find vengeance by destroying all of us. But without your anger, you're weak. Underneath your fear, you're fragile. Unarmed, you are merely a man." She leaps forward, knocks him off his feet, catches him before he falls, buries her teeth in his throat, and drinks.

Nick struggles. He squirms. It's less painful than he'd expected. More erotic. When his friends died in the cemetery, when his parents were slaughtered, those creatures had been ruthless and frenzied. Lady Chandra isn't anything like that. She's rough, yes, but as she promised, she's careful. Delicate.

He tries to fight, but every ounce of blood she sucks from him is an ounce of resistance lost. Every moment in her arms discredits all he's ever believed himself to be. He's not merely being fed upon, not merely being transformed, he's being humiliated and shamed and dishonored.

Nick Hunter tries to defy her, but in the end all he can do is endure. If he's capable, after, if he's still in control of his own facilities, maybe this will give him an edge in his war.

Lady Chandra pulls away from him. He's sprawled across the floor, in her arms, staring up at her, feeling weaker than he's ever felt before. She offers her wrist. She's cut it open. Blood doesn't pour out, merely seeps, but she thrusts the opening to his mouth and says, "Drink, my little hunter. This is only your first taste."

6.

The way to the stars is long and tight. The tunnels away from the underground lake twist and turn. Some are hand cut, but others are natural. These aren't mineshafts but actual caves. They're narrow, and often too low to allow anything but crawling. This doesn't slow the scavenger; she moves on all fours naturally. For Jack Harlow, however, the going is rough.

Outside of the scavenger's lair, there are very few sources of light. In the absolute darkness, however, Jack can still see. Not well. Not in detail. But he can see the outline and shapes of things. He sees where the rocks jut out. He sees how far ahead the scavenger gets before she stops, exasperated, and waits for him to catch up.

They're crawling up and down. Jack has no concept of depth. He doesn't know how far he fell, or how low he'd already been.

While they crawl, the scavenger insists on stories. "Something interesting this time," she says. "Something you did or saw or heard or something."

Jack Harlow is no storyteller. "I once met a man who was a ghost."

"A spectral ghost, all dead and deceased, an afterimage of what was?"

"No, he was sentient."

"Intelligent?"

"I wouldn't go that far. He was lonely."

"Because he was a ghost?"

"Yes."

"Couldn't he just kill someone and make another ghost?"

"I don't think that's how ghosts work."

"Don't you know?" the scavenger asks.

"No, I don't."

"What kind of storyteller are you?"

"I'm not," he reminds her.

"If I took the dog, I would've gotten his weapons. I bet there was another knife there." She had claimed the knife Jack had managed to take from him during their fall. He doesn't even remember how that happened. He thinks it was after they hit the water. He thinks he got lucky.

"So this lonely ghost man," the scavenger says. "What was his name?"

"I don't know."

"How can you not know?"

"I didn't ask."

"Why not?"

"Listen," Jack says. "I don't know a lot about telling stories, but I do know they go a lot easier if you stop asking so many questions."

"I wouldn't have to ask questions if you told it right."

"What's the right way?"

"You start with a hero," the scavenger says. "You start with a villain. A conflict."

"There's not always a conflict."

"Then it's not a good story. Now shush."

They enter a wider, more open area. It's not huge. Jack can see stalagmites and stalactites – he doesn't know which drop from the ceiling and which rise from the floor, but together they make the side of the cavern look like a giant mouth.

If it was actually a mouth of something, Jack Harlow, DarkWalker, would know.

Spiders crawl over those teeth, spiders the size of his fist, and in the darkness, other things hide or cower or sleep. Some are wounded. Some are corpses. Not the animated kind of corpses, but actual dead things that had once been something else. There's a large number of those in this cavern.

"See, there's a story," the scavenger says, whispering. "There was a hero, and there was a villain, and they fought until they were both dead, and this is where their followers ended up."

"Really?"

"Doesn't have to be true," she says.

They go around one of the corpses. It's fresh and fetid, and Jack wishes he wasn't so accustomed to the odors of the dead. The stench is strong. "How much more?"

The scavenger grins back at him over her shoulder, then hurries forward, into another of those tight caves. This is even tighter than the previous, and its rocky protrusions snag at his clothes and skin.

"Did you know the ghost man when he was alive?"

"I didn't."

"How did you meet?"

"In a bar."

"You were drinking?"

"He wanted to," Jack admits, "but it's a bit difficult to drink when you're incorporeal."

She giggles. It's light, almost childlike, but quick. "And why didn't you know his name?"

"Same reason I don't know yours," Jack says. "He didn't tell me."

She stops. She looks back at him. "I lied."

"About the stars?"

"No. About me." She starts moving again. "I've never had a name. Always been a scavenger. Never anything else, more or less, so that's what I've always been called. I ain't got a name, not a right one."

After squeezing through another tight section, Jack asks, "Would you like a name?"

She shakes her head. "No need of one down here."

"When I tell your story," Jack says, "how will I know what to call you?"

"I'm the scavenger," she says. "Always been enough, always will be." She slows down as she reaches the end of this tunnel. It opens up onto something wide and deep. She steps gingerly to one side, back against the wall, arms outstretched. The ledge is maybe a foot wide. Jack cannot see how far a fall it is. He hears wings flapping, not just a single set, perhaps an entire colony of bats. Precarious is only the first word that comes to mind.

"How far?" Jack asks.

"Don't stop now," she says. She's sliding carefully across the ledge. It seems sturdy enough, though she's probably half his weight and twice as agile.

He hugs the wall. It seems safer. He doesn't have the same musculature in his legs as the scavenger. She's a climber. He's – well, to put a fine point on it, a kind of *walker*.

It's maybe a dozen yards. It seems like forever and it takes that long. Something flies near enough that he feels its wind. Something small. It doesn't touch him.

At the end of the ledge, at a platform that marks the bottom of a set of stairs, the scavenger extends a hand to help guide him. She touches his back, presses him against the wall, urges him forward. When he reaches the edge, she whispers, "You're an expert."

"The stars," Jack says.

"I like you," the scavenger says. "You're not like the dogs."

"What are the dogs like?"

She shrugs. "Nasty. They bite. You were a dog, I would've shoved you into the chasm, listening to you cry as you fell and fell and fell."

"How far down does it go?"

"All the way."

That seems reasonable. Jack turns to the stairway. The steps are uneven, smoothed by time and use, dangerous and slippery. There's no light whatsoever, but he can see this. He hesitates. Looks back down the chasm. "Is there another way down?"

"No." Too quick. She takes a breath. "Yes. There are ways down. But there's no bottom to the chasm. It just goes forever until the end."

"The end of what?"

"The end of time."

Jack shakes his head. "It's not *that* deep. There's something in the dark down there."

"Then we better go, before it eats us."

Jack hesitates just a moment longer, even as the scavenger takes the steps two at a time. Her sense of balance is as perfect as any cat's, and his is nearly as good. He chases after her, upwards, toward the stars.

The staircase curves only slightly, and emerges at the bottom of a vast cavern. It might be as big as the lake they'd left behind. The ground declines toward the center. The ceiling rises. And set in the ceiling are the stars: gems, perhaps, quartz and mica, veins of silver and sulfur, pearls set into the ceiling, thousands of these making a collection of stars and constellations, not too dissimilar to the actual night sky. He recognizes the Big

Dipper and Orion and other shapes, even if they're imprecise.

The stars cover the ceiling and the walls. He reaches out, touches a raw chunk of garnet star. The red comes from inside it. Nearby mica stars are like gold, and there are golden stars as well. Platinum. Mercury. Hematite. Iron. Sapphire. Not all of these are naturally found here, not all of these are indigenous, not all of these were brought down and placed by the hands of men, gods, or beasts.

Jack touches another star, this one gold. It pops out of the rock and into his hands. It's a coin, a double eagle from 1907 (the coin says MCMVII), Lady Liberty on one side, *United States* and *Twenty Dollars* engraved on the other. The edges are rough, but not terrible.

The scavenger purrs as she walks around Jack and her tail curls around her legs. "As promised," she says, "I've brought you to the stars."

The stars are bright, even brilliant, in the absolute darkness under the mines of Silver Blade. Jack's breath catches in his throat. He slips the coin into his pocket, his own personal star. "I don't understand."

"The stars have always been here," the scavengers said.

"These have not all always been here," Jack says.

"Maybe no. But stars pop into and out of existence all the time. Everybody knows that."

"These aren't the stars I meant."

The scavenger shakes her head. "These are the stars I know. These are the only stars there are."

"No," Jack says, taking her by the shoulders. "In the night sky, there are stars, stars like these, but they're up in the sky and we cannot reach them, we cannot pluck them from the wall with our fingers. They provide light, maybe to other planets, other worlds, other peoples, even. I meant the stars shining down on the earth, stars that might guide a ship, stars that would say I'm not buried under tons of rock and dirt."

The scavenger looks scared. Hesitantly, she adds, "And metal."

"I need to get outside."

She shakes her head. "There is no outside."

7.

Naomi wakes. This time, she's fully aware and fully alert. The flickering fire provides only a little light. No one's standing over her, but she hears the animals playing with each other, roughhousing like puppies, yipping, growling, falling over each other.

Without moving, she assesses the damage. Her shoulder throbs. It should. It had been gouged. She touches her ring and middle fingers to each other. They work. She feels them. That's a good sign. Or they're phantom limbs. Warmth flows through her blood, warmth she's not accustomed to. Something the woman did, something she did with her own blood, over which she has extraordinary control. Color. Intensity. Reaction.

Slowly, carefully and quietly, Naomi turns her head toward the light. The woman with the translucent skin and green veins stands over the fire with her back to Naomi. She's leaning close, whispering words into the flames, listening for their responses. Naomi almost hears responses, and almost understands them. Her arm is still attached. The wound is raw and bloody, but there's a white liquid smeared over much of it, and the pain is far less than it should be. The pain should be enough to kill her. There shouldn't be anything left of her collarbone or shoulder, none of the muscles, none of the tendons. Her nerves should be dangling loose and burning.

She doesn't know the woman's name, so she calls her, "Vèt." *Green.*

The woman turns and smiles. Her smile is full of teeth. The color in her veins intensifies. She says words. They're still foreign words, they're still beyond translation, but Naomi understands the meaning. Vèt is pleased she's alive. She comes closer, examines the wound, prods it with her fingers. Naomi feels the pressure, but not the pain. She secretes drops of white and blue from her fingers. They land on the wound.

Naomi turns her head back and sighs. She will live. She will heal. She doesn't, however, know the cost. It will be high. Costs always are.

There's no point in running. She doesn't know how to get back anymore. She doesn't know how deep into the mines she is. This is Silver Blade, and it seems this is the last place she will know.

But Vèt has other plans. She whispers to Naomi, whispers directly into her ear and into her mind. The words are unclear, but images form anyhow. Intention. Direction. North? The direction is north, but that's just a word, a symbol on a map, the top of the compass rose. What it really means is up. *Up.* Out of this shallow city. Out of the darkness.

She says, "I'm not alone down here."

This causes Vèt to pause. It's brief. She says something. She indicates the animals, the three of them, sitting now obediently, eyes sharp. She indicates the brazier, the twin fire figures, who are not quite alive and not entirely complete. She indicates herself by touching the center of her chest, her heart. She indicates Naomi. Then she closes two fists in front of her and touches the butts of those fists to each other. She holds them there a moment, in front of her chest, then lifts them and splays her fingers and separates her hands. Up, out, and away. She says something else, but by now she knows words are pointless. She hesitates a moment, touches the center of Naomi's chest, and enunciates, very slowly and with utter deliberation, one syllable at a time: "*El. A. Vate. Or.*"

CHAPTER SIX

1.

They exchange blood and kisses and delirium. Nick's head swims. His senses aren't his. She's in complete control. He never expected to die this way. He always knew there'd be teeth, but he expected pain. He expected glory. He doesn't even know what this is.

It's a pit. That's not a surprise. It's a pit under the earth. That's not a surprise either. And he dies in the arms of a vampire. Up until this point, it's like the universe doesn't know how to make a surprise. But the rest of it, the ease of it and the softness, the gentleness with which Lady Chandra treats him, he never expected.

And there'll be no one to put him down when he rises. Oh, and he *will* rise, he's already something other than himself. His blood is hot, as much hers as his own. He's bled, and he's drunk, and he tries to block it out. But he also tries to absorb every detail, every nuance, so that he can maybe prevent this in the future. Or perform it.

There are moments of resistance, when his instincts take hold and he struggles, when he tries to break away from Lady Chandra's grip. There are moments of complete dreaming, when he sees his partner, Diane, and his trainer, Chris, like a god descending into the pit to sever all the heads.

There are moments of pain. And there are moments of complete, utter clarity, when he looks into Lady Chandra's eyes and sees the vicious glee inside them. This is a great victory for the vampires. This is a great failing for the hunters.

There are others out there, with knives and guns, fighting the good fight. Preachers and sinners alike struggling to turn back the festering tide of evil. He was never alone, although he always was.

"You'll be stronger than you ever were," she says, her voice like a mother's to an infant. "You'll be quicker and more agile, and you'll be able to see in the dark. Your eyesight should already be changing, and your sense of hearing, and your sense of smell. You were a hunter, once, but now you will be hunted. *Reviled.* You will be hated by the very people you tried to protect. And you will drink, little hunter, because otherwise you would suffer, and you would suffer a long, long time without the blood."

At some point, Nick closes his eyes. He dies. He feels his heart fail to beat. The blood stops in his veins. It's brief. It's only a moment. But it's the most important moment he's ever experienced. There's no light, no dark, no sign of anything outside of this pit, not because there isn't anything but because he's already destined for something else. Even in death, he tightens his fists, he grabs a chunk of Lady Chandra's hair. There's no dignity in this death.

"You should be feeling the potency of my blood in your veins. You should find a new vigor, a new intensity, a new everything. You are mine and I am yours, little hunter. This is how you love, as a vampire, little hunter. This is how we make love. This is how we multiply." It's all whispers. Promises. Threats. "This is how we conquer."

"I never wanted this," Nick says, now that his heart beats again, now that sensation returns to the tips of his fingers and his tongue and his head. He sees Lady Chandra as he's never seen anyone before, and he feels a great affinity toward her, something he never expected, something close to love. It may be artificial. It may be a lie. But it's thorough and undeniable.

Lady Chandra smiles and says, "And yet."

2.

Jack Harlow sits on a rock underneath the cavern stars. He sits, and he stares at them, and he finally looks at the scavenger. "You're wrong," he says. "I'm *from* outside. I'm from under the stars, the real stars in the real sky."

"That," the scavenger says, "would be a story."

"I was born in a massive city. New York. And I grew up on Long Island."

"What's an island?"

"Land," Jack says, "surrounded by water."

"Like the rock in the middle of the lake," the scavenger says.

Jack remembers no such thing. "Sure. Just like that. Except this was a large island, large enough for cities, and I lived there until I was seventeen."

"What happened?"

"I...I guess you can say I ran away."

"Really?"

"I learned something about myself," Jack says, "something I didn't understand, and I left. I didn't know it then, but I left to find out who I was."

"So who are you?"

Jack sighed and shook his head. "I don't know."

"What's it like, the sky?" the scavenger asks. "I've always thought it was a myth. And I know you're just telling a story. But tell me, what's it like."

"It's big," Jack says. "Wide open."

"Like this room?"

"Much, much bigger," Jack says. "It stretches forever in every direction."

"Nothing stretches forever, except maybe time, and I ain't too sure about that, either."

Jack taps the rock beneath him with a fist. "There's no walls. No ceiling. There's only sky. During the day, it's blue, a brilliant creamy blue that goes on forever. And at night, it's black, velvet, and there are stars like these stars, but so far away it would take lifetimes to get to them."

"And the moon?" the scavenger asks. "Is that a real thing?"

"It is."

"Made of cheese?"

"No. Rock."

"Like here."

Jack shakes his head. "Not like here at all."

"And you want to get back there, to where you hang stars too far away to reach, and where there's a moon you can't eat, and there's nowhere to hide."

After a brief hesitation, Jack says, "I've spent my life hiding. There's plenty of places to hide."

The scavenger steps directly before him, arm's length away. Standing, she can't be more than four feet flat. The irises of her eyes are slits, like a cat or a snake. She's young. This is all the life she's ever known. "That's a much better story than the acheri. Does that mean other places, like Boston, those are real places, above the ground, outside and in the open and under the sky like the place you're from?"

"Yes."

"And we can walk there?"

"It might take a while to walk, but sure," Jack says. "I have a car."

"You say some strange things, Jack Harlow of the sky."

"I have to go back."

She shakes her head. "They say we can climb, we can rise, we can go higher than we are, but there's no stories, none, that say we can go through the top and see the sky. I mean, there's stories, but they're all false, and everybody knows it. But to go up? From here? Unless you can fly, you can't."

"I can't."

"We can go down," she says. "I can bring you to the lower deeps. To the deep city, even. And then, if we can find the right story or storyteller, we might find another way to climb."

"You don't have to go," Jack says.

"What, I should wait for something awesome to drop down the pit again?" She shakes her head. "It's not like that down here. You, you're a little bit awesome, and I like you, and I'm glad I salvaged you, but I ain't about to let you take your stories away until I've been properly recompensed, you got that?"

"Sure," Jack says. "I got that."

"The deep city waits," the scavenger says. "You might want to wish upon a star before we go. There's a good chance you'll never see the stars again."

"Maybe not these stars," Jack says. "But I have every intention to see the real ones."

3.

Naomi sits up. She opens and closes her fist. There's pressure inside her shoulder, and the wound looks terrible, but everything seems to work. She's ginger about it, though. She doesn't try doing shoulder rolls or reaching over her head. A little bit at a time. She doesn't know what to expect. She might damage it more. Whatever's masking the pain might stop working.

What she's gathered is simple enough: they're trapped at this level, stuck, held, and Vèt wants to rise higher. Maybe she wants to get outside. Their method of communication is imprecise at best.

It's probably too late to warn Jack Harlow. Whatever it is they sent him down here for, he's faced it, or is facing it now. The hunter friend he seeks was probably a lie. A lure. This was a trap, and Lance Turner led them straight into it. When she gets to the surface, with or without Jack Harlow, she'll walk into the inn, right past Brina and Burke if she has to, and rip Lance's heart from his ribcage. She'll squeeze it and crush it before his eyes stop transmitting to his brain. His suffering will be short, but then he'll be dead. She might have to fight her way out of Silver Blade. She might be able to do it, if Vèt fights with her, if Vèt sics her pets on their opponents, if Vèt can direct those two dancing flames to fight.

For the moment, though, the flames dance in the brazier, some sort of Latin dance, a tango, back and forth with each other. Vèt watches them and repeats her mantra, over and over again, each time giving the flames a bit more strength, a bit more power.

If there's a timeframe to Vèt's plans and intentions, Naomi doesn't know it. The elevator cage is at the level above. Presumably, it only comes down when it's sent. She's beginning to understand something of the hierarchy here. The higher you go, the easier your existence. The mines of Silver Blade go deeper. She doesn't want to know how deep. This was never meant to be a rescue mission. There may be hundreds, even thousands, of creatures of darkness living down here, and they're probably very dangerous. They were put here for a reason.

Or they came from here. What if this hole in the earth is the source of darkness, if somewhere below there's an infernal cauldron from which the demons of the earth have risen, where the first spirits were ripped from the bodies of men, where vampires and werewolves were created, where the bogeyman first drew breath and the goblins first drew blood, where perhaps even dragons were forged.

She doesn't know what Vèt is or what she'll do when she reaches the surface. It might be a very, very bad idea. But Naomi isn't ready to die, and the woman with the translucent flesh and the volatile blood hasn't been entirely malevolent. She might bring hell to earth, she might unleash demons and monsters and fiends, she might set out to conquer and annihilate. She might enslave all the men of the world or simply slaughter them. But right now, from this vantage point, from within the shallow city of Silver Blade, Vèt is a prisoner seeking freedom. Who is Naomi to deny her that? Right now, Naomi seeks the same thing.

Naomi gives her arm a better, more dangerous test. She puts both hands palms down on the rock slab she sits on and pushes up, lifting her butt, supporting all her weight with her arms. The pressure builds. Tendrils of pain shoot through her shoulder. She breaks a sweat with the effort. She's panting as she settles back down.

Vèt is looking at her, scowling, making some sort of expression with her face and teeth. It might be disapproval. It might be amusement. It might be something so close to both Naomi can't read it. But she smiles herself. The arm functions. It supports her. She won't be able to climb the elevator shaft yet, but she didn't lose it.

Vèt moves toward her, offering something in a closed hand. Naomi holds out her hand to accept it. When Vèt speaks, the words are foreign but the tone is one of uncertainty. She drops a microchip into Naomi's hand.

Not just any microchip. This is the thing Jack Harlow's father had put in her, probably a tracer, definitely a remotely-operated release mechanism for quick-acting poison. So small a thing. So deadly. Such a violation. Naomi examines it for a moment. It's a green rectangle smaller than her fingernail. The symbols on it might be another language, and they are, but an internal language, a series of codes. There's two small dots of liquid, less than a drop of either, separated from each other but ready to react. Naomi reaches down – it's an effort, she's still weak – to pick up a piece of rock. She doesn't know what it is, except that it's solid and sharp at the corner. She sets the chip down and grinds it down with the rock. When the liquids combine, they smoke. There's barely any sound, just the rock in her hand against the rock on the floor, not any louder than the fire, and a brief sizzle as the combined liquids, the poisons, work their acidic selves into the ground. It's only a moment before she's done. The poison makes the smallest possible hole. She's pulverized the chip, and she feels better for it.

She leans back, lays down again, smiling. Vèt watches all this without a word. Darkness closes in from the edges of Naomi's vision. This time, she rejects oblivion.

4.

Nick Hunter, vampire, wakes to the night. It's a glorious feeling. Every ache he's kept, every pain he's endured, has calmed to nothingness. He feels whole, from his fingers to his toes, from his head to his heart. He's conscious of every square inch of his body. He feels the stirring of the air. He smells the dirt and the rocks, and the blood of his vampire mistress. The air temperature is half a degree cooler at his ankle than at his wrist. He's maintained his scars. They're the history of him, how he got to be who he is today, but the heat of them is gone. He hears distant dripping water, the pulse of Lady Chandra beside him, the pulse of the dogs above pretending to guard this pit. He reaches out with his senses, able to understand the shape of the mines, the deposits of silver and sulfur intertwined in the rock. His clothes are rough. His weapons crude. And his eyes – he sees in the dark like he's never seen, colors he never expected were real. Lady Chandra's eyes are a kaleidoscope. She smiles as he sits up, independently, no longer in need of the support. He says, "I never knew."

"You never would have."

He touches the floor of the pit. Rock. Dirt. Sweat. Blood. People have died in this pit. He scents the echoes of them. He can't reach far enough to see what the queen is doing on her throne, but the perfume of her – so small a word – her scents linger in many places.

"It can be overwhelming, at first," Lady Chandra says. "And the thirst – are you thirsty, my little hunter?"

He isn't thinking about thirst or hunger or need. He's lost in his senses, exploring, pushing at the boundaries. But now that she's said it, there is a thirst, a yearning, a diabolical need deep inside him. He licks his lips. He meets the multi-chromatic eyes of his lover and says, "Yes."

"Go," she says, urging him upwards. "A meal awaits."

Nick nods. He rises to his feet. Strength courses through him like he's never felt. Power. Urgency. He leaps. He overshoots the rim of the pit, smashes the ceiling, cracks one of the rotting timbers that holds the earth over them. It's already weak. He knew it before. The mines will not last. The caves underneath – there are caves, he can smell them, the difference in ambience. The shallow city of Silver Blade smells of rot and decay and decadence and death. But below that, there are the caves, and the deep city, fresher and more serene, and more mysterious.

He stumbles at the edge of the pit. Four dogs sit there playing cards. The cards are old, torn and ragged. They play for bits of metal, silver and sulfur and arsenic. They move fast. Nick moves faster. He grabs one by the throat, lifts the dog off its feet with one hand. It's hardly an effort. Like lifting a heavy dictionary or Bible. He's crushing its windpipe without even meaning to.

The others lunge forward, weapons drawn. He swings the dying dog at them, smashes its body against them, disrupts whatever intention they thought they had. He dives into them, tearing with fingernails sharp as steel, ripping chunks of flesh from the beasts like cotton candy. Their blood is fetid, dirty and undesirable, but he needs the blood. He's never been so thirsty.

"Careful," Lady Chandra whispers in his ear, calming his berserker rage. "The silver will hurt you, don't forget that. And their blood is...distasteful."

"It's rancid," he says.

"Oh, it is. They're easy enough to hunt and kill, for

practice or for fun, but they're not what you really want to feed on."

Nick takes a huge lungful of air. "The *queen*."

Lady Chandra whispers so quietly, no one and nothing else can hear, not even if rock demons press their ears to the mine walls. "The *seer* has reigned long enough, I think. I believe it's time for a new queen."

Of course. Nick grins. It's an evil, wicked, nasty grin, and he knows it. The Lady Chandra, the other vampires, all the other beasts and creatures in this shallow city, have been subservient because of the power structure. She's played her role long enough. The Lady Chandra is, after all, a rightful queen, noble by birth, a lady in every sense of the word. The seer, the *pretender*, the *usurper*, she's old now and weak, and she should be destroyed.

"First," Lady Chandra says, "we need to get you properly fed."

Nick says. "There's something close."

"That's me you scent," she says, kissing his throat. "My blood won't sustain you."

"Something else."

"Show me."

This highest level of the shallow city is divided into three sections. The first is empty, an entryway of sorts, which leads to the queen's brothel and throne room. Then there's the queen's rooms, a series of chambers and corridors for her and her chosen. The rest of it, a series of shafts dug by the hands of men, with mine carts that have rusted into place, with areas so unstable, the ceiling holds itself up only by momentum. Miles of corridors and passageways, and a half dozen pits, all guarded, all leading to lower levels. The things that try to rise are generally destroyed. The air moves because the creatures here move. And they are all creatures, each and every one, whether predator or prey.

Nick used to believe he was at the top of that food chain. He never was. For years, he hunted weaker, malformed vampires, beasts without reason, without identity, without substance. They never deserved to become that. He's been ending their miseries. Granting them relief and release. The higher vampires, like Jia Lia, like the man he hadn't killed in Richmond, like the Lady Chandra behind him, are different. They'd been transformed with purpose, sometimes malice, sometimes love.

Nick leads the way through these tunnels, through the remnants of a collapse, to a colony of survivors who thought they were separate and protected. The crevices and cracks in the rock are easy to slip past. He doesn't disturb a pebble. A dozen, no more, live here, quiet but still vicious, still things of the dark. He finds one at the outskirts. Takes him.

The prey never has a chance to cry out.

Nick cracks his neck and drinks. Hungrily. Greedily. Messily. He drinks till he is full, until the blood that remains seeps out of the wounds in a trickle.

"You'll develop patience," Lady Chandra tells him, "and technique. You won't need to brutalize them when you can seduce. When they come to you, when they give themselves willingly – the blood is all the sweeter, my little hunter."

"Have you always been Lady?" Nick asks.

"Not always, no."

"Has there never been a Lord?"

She smiles. "Once."

"Is he dead?" She doesn't answer immediately, so Nick asks, "How did you end up here, in Silver Blade?"

"A man. Jonathan Harlow."

"I know that name."

"It was long ago," she says. "When I was young and fresh and unskilled."

"And now?"

"And now," she says, her grin showing all her teeth, "you've awakened something in me. I didn't know, I didn't even expect it. I've been serving the seer – Tania – for almost as long as I can remember. But my days under the earth are done."

"We can just leave," Nick says.

"We can. But vengeance is so much more fun."

5.

The scavenger leads Jack Harlow out of the starry cavern the way they entered, down the stairs, deeper into the dark. At the landing, rather than returning along the perilous ledge, she turns the other way. A stairway leads down the side of the rock wall. It's not a neat, even, orderly staircase, nor even the time-worn and dangerous steps that lead to the stars. It's footholds roughly hewn into the rock, each one unique, some missing, some further apart than they should be, some too close together.

"Balance," the scavenger says, "ain't a problem for me. Is it for you?"

"It won't be," Jack says, but of course he doesn't know. This isn't the easiest balancing trick he's ever tried to pull off. It's not like standing on the edge of an office building while a vampire suckles at your throat and holds you steady in the wind.

There is no wind in Silver Blade.

The steps are little more that deviations in the smooth wall. Every movement is precarious. A sense of vertigo threatens at the edges of Jack's head. But he finds he's sure-footed, he hits every step perfectly, and he holds onto the occasional handholds someone was kind enough to carve.

At the last step, the scavenger leaps sideways. It's maybe a meter to the ledge, to actual ground. She lands, crouches, and looks back. "The last step is gone. Probably someone who didn't know how to walk, how to hug the wall, how to *stand*. Probably fell to an ugly and slow death."

"Slow?"

"Bottomless. He'll fall forever. Now jump."

Jack's on the last step. He can't turn to face the ledge head on, so he's got to jump to the side. Off a ledge that's smaller than his foot. With one foot dangling. He takes a breath, bends his knee, and pushes. For a moment, he's suspended in the air, between the step and the ledge, over a bottom chasm – he knows there's no such thing – a superhero in flight or a suicide falling to their death. Both simultaneously. He wants to close his eyes, but he's not willing to surrender his life to hope and chance. He hits the edge of the ledge with one foot – not both. He pitches his weight forward but angles back with the effort. The scavenger grabs him by the throat and chest, claws extended, and yanks him forward.

They fall, together, and the scavenger turns them bodily away from the edge so that they end up on their shoulders instead of over the side.

"We ain't even begun," she says. "You can't fall yet."

On the other side of the ledge, there's a proper staircase. It doesn't descend into the abyss, but into the rock. They're thoroughly surrounded by solid rock.

There's still no light source.

"Storytime," she says. "This one better be good."

"Maybe you should tell a story," Jack says.

"I salvaged and saved you. You owe me."

"How did you end up down here?"

"Ha! That ain't a story. I was born here, me and my sisters and brothers, the lot of us, here in the dark."

"You've always been here?"

"I ain't never seen Boston, if that's what you mean. Or an endless sky."

"Trees?"

"Roots."

"Cities?"

"The shallow and the deep."

"But you know about Boston?"

"I know about a lot of places. Paris. Prague. El Dorado. Xanadu. Alexandria."

"Those aren't all real places."

"Neither is Boston. I ain't never seen a one. But their stories persist, and for as long as there are stories, there are cities. I've always believed that."

"But you haven't, not really."

"Belief," the scavenger says, "ain't the same as knowing."

The stairs twist and turn and eventually come to a fork. Steps continue down to the left, and more steeply to the right. The scavenger doesn't even seem to make a decision; she goes right.

As they descend, the stairs cease to exist, becoming less artificial and more natural, so that they're walking not on stairs but on an uneven decline of rocky floor. These aren't mines anymore, but natural caves. Clumps of stalactites and stalagmites line the stairs. Abruptly, they widen, and the ceiling raises above them. They are not alone in the cavern. Kobolds and goblins watch from safe alcoves a dozen feet above the ground. In places, it's not like stairs at all, but a rolling field – if the field had been laid with rock and given walls and ceiling. The openings renew a sense of claustrophobia in Jack, which seems counterintuitive. The air here has never seen the sun or the moon, but it's not stale like in the mine. It's clean. Fresh. Doesn't even smell of death anymore.

"They know what we want," the scavenger says. "It's easier to descend than rise. Some of us have spent years, most of our lives, rising to where we are. The higher we go, the closer we get to god."

"You believe that?"

"Some do."

"Which god?" Jack asks.

She doesn't answer that. "There's plenty in the deep city will let you go on past them, if you're going down. Like it frees up space up top for them. It doesn't and it don't. But they'll kill you, if they think you're cutting ahead of them. There ain't no line. There's just – there's just us, all of us, everyone and everything here. I do well enough. But there are predators. Monsters."

"Where I'm from, all of us would be considered monsters," Jack says.

"Where I'm from," the scavenger tells him, "no one would say that. So, tell me a story. About where you're from."

"Long Island?"

"You got trees and water and stuff?"

"Yes. Woods and lakes and the ocean."

She shudders visibly. "That's the water that goes forever, right? The riptides that come in and steal you from the earth and drown you and bash your body against sharp rocks."

"It's not exactly like that," Jack says.

"Only stories I know about the oceans, there's things bigger than the lake that'll devour ships and cities and don't even notice us."

"There's things like that everywhere, I think."

"You been on the ocean?"

"I have."

"You ever see one of them? The great old ones?"

Jack thinks about that. He's seen things, even things he cannot explain. "Not that I know of."

"You know what I think? I think there's old ones under the earth. Under the deep city. Waiting."

"Waiting for what?"

She shakes her head. "Unimaginable and indescribable things?"

"I don't know that I believe that," Jack says.

"You're supposed to be telling me a story about the ocean."

"I thought you wanted a story about the island."

"Islands float on the ocean, right? What else did you see? Icebergs? Leviathans? Krill?"

"I saw a dolphin once."

"Will you take me to the ocean? When we get above the shallow city?"

Around the next turn, the cavern grows, and it's no longer a tunnel but a massive opening under which narrow hovels lean against each other, alleys run between structures built from the rock and metal around them. The ceiling is marbleized and far above them. A bat drifts overhead, its wingspan easily ten feet or more, the red glow of its eyes visible from where the scavenger has led Jack.

It's a promenade, with tiered steps leading down to the main section of the city. And it is a city – small, perhaps, but probably the largest city ever built underground. There are hundreds of little houses, numerous tunnels leading away from the center, walls, statues and grotesques. One of these crawls along the wall above Jack, staring down at him. There's commotion, but much less so than in the marketplace of the shallow city.

"Welcome," the scavenger says, "to the deep city."

Jack simply stares. There are windows made, not of glass, but of thin, sheer sheets of rock. There's metal.

There are gems. Pits and braziers contain small fires. There's an orc crouched under the bridge eating meat. There's a *bridge*. It runs from one rock wall to another. It might even be natural. There are massive stone columns. It looks like a deranged surrealist put this city together, banging architectural styles together at random.

"The deep city," the scavenger says, "has always been here. They came and built the shallow city and dug out their precious metals and made weapons to kill us and enslave us. They called the shallow city Silver Blade, but they didn't know we were already here. I was born here, my mother was born here, her mother before her, a hundred generations or a thousand, I don't know."

Jack doesn't know what to say or think. "What is this place?"

"Home." Then she sighs. "Until I rose up to the lake, and I set about scavenging there, between the deep and shallow cities. Until *now*, Jack Harlow, when you'll take me from here to the sky and the ocean and Boston."

CHAPTER SEVEN

1.

The deep city below Silver Blade spreads before Jack Harlow like a revelation. The walls are crooked rock and sheets of metal. There are eyes at every corner, shadows at every light. Braziers line the street like street lamps. The smoke drifts up and out. The ceiling is veined, and in some sections there are paintings, or parts of paintings, whether either the artist didn't finish or time has played critic. As the scavenger steps towards this, more and more people, creatures, and beasts notice the new arrival. There are reptilian men and creatures with rocky skin and even an ogre. He's met one of those before.

A stream meanders through the city. It moves slow, but it moves, and in the water blind fish dart away from the hooks and talons of creatures lounging along the shore. It's almost a canal, the way it snakes between the structures. There are arches and spires. There's even a building that appears to be a kind of church. Jack knows this in the same way he knows so many other things. The dark is a mystery to most, but to Jack Harlow it's a blossoming enigma. He knows things, and then knows he's wrong about those things. The breadth of his knowledge remains elusive.

Walls are painted in bright colors, though in the flickering firelight everything is gray and tinted red. A nearby window shade closes. There's the sound of metal on metal, like a sewage grate closing. Footsteps approach, even if Jack cannot immediately see where they come from. Shadows drift between the shadows.

The Mayor approaches. Jack Harlow, DarkWalker, knows this is the mayor because his sight, his intuition, his gift and power, tells him this, just as it named the scavenger. She scuttles closer to him, an arm out as if to protect the deep city from him. The mayor is flanked by mole men, two humanoid figures with big wide eyes and no noses. They're not identical. One is scaled, the other's skin is more akin to dirt in tone and texture. They could crush heads in their hands like tomatoes. They remain half a step behind the Mayor, who is of course something else, something even more powerful.

"I salvaged him," the scavenger says, hissing. "He's mine."

The Mayor ignores her. "You've come from above."

Jack looks around. Other creatures are watching. Trolls. Gnomes. Dwarves. Phantoms and phantasms. It sounds like a statement, not a question, so Jack says nothing and lets the Mayor continue. "I can smell the greenery still on you. You were sent here to die."

"Perhaps."

The Mayor shakes his head. "Not my decision to make. I shan't be killing you, if that eases your mind any."

"Not much."

"You're a watcher," the Mayor says. "You're not used to this. The proximity – maybe – but not the numbers. I should warn you, this is as deep as we get."

"It goes deeper," the scavenger says.

"This is as deep as anyone wants to go," the Mayor says. "You've travelled a long way. You must be tired."

"No," Jack says. "Anxious to continue."

"Continue to where?"

The scavenger's shaking her head, but Jack says, "Upward."

"Ascension is rare," the Mayor says. "The gates are guarded or collapsed." He smiles like a politician. It puts a bad taste in Jack's mouth. "But you're not merely a watcher, are you? You're not a watcher at all." He reaches out, hesitates, asks, "May I shake your hand?"

Jack stares down at the offered hand. The Mayor, whatever he might be, may have the strength to grind the bones in his hand, but why be so roundabout? Why not just crack open his skull here without the pretense? Jack extends his hand and shakes. The grip is firm but not overpowering. The Mayor closes his other hand over Jack's. "Yes, the repulsion is strong, but I have felt stronger." He lets go. "Tell me, is the shallow city as it was?"

"How was it?" Jack asks.

"*Shallow.*" The Mayor nods. "Yes, and depraved. We've been closing the tunnels to the shallow city, cutting them off, destroying them when they venture deeper."

"Why?" Jack asks.

"Rotten," the Mayor says. "The mine, the city, the *people* – if you call them that." He clears his throat. "You don't happen to be an emissary of the shallow city, are you?"

"No."

"Nor the watchers," the Mayor says. "So as I said, they sent you to die."

"You've already established that," Jack says.

"Yes, yes, of course. What I mean to say is, you're here alone, without support. That is, I would think, a mistake."

2.

Nick Hunter, vampire, stands over the remnants of a pair of dogs. He doesn't drink. This is pure vengeance. He holds the heart of one in his hands. He hears every drop of blood falling from it. He smells its pale coppery scent. The dogs are bastardizations of something greater that came before, warped and twisted by generations under the silver. Abominations, is what they are. The more hideously deformed patrol the lower levels of the shallow city. Up here, where the queen might see them, she's chosen only those that are easy to look at. Faces that haven't been broken by inbreeding.

"The werewolf," Lady Chandra tells him, "was once a mighty creature. Strong. Proud. There are, of course, variations, off-shoots, mistakes. But mostly, they're noble, they're loyal, they're pack animals. But down here, under the watchful eye of the seer, their breed has gone to rot."

'They would fight *with* us," Nick suggests.

She smiles generously. "You think we need allies?"

"No."

"They're all hers. So they'll all suffer with her."

"She's moving."

"Of course she's moving."

He feels the change in the environment. He listens deeply. He hears her footsteps. Her breathing. They're close, even if walls of rock separate them. He leans toward the wall, dropping the dog's heart and absently licking his fingers. "She knows."

"Of course she knows," Lady Chandra says. "I don't know exactly what she is or how or why, but she sees into the hearts of us. She sees into our souls. She knows what we plan before we do."

Nick looks a question at Lady Chandra. If the queen seer knows, how is it that the Lady Chandra was able to hide her intentions?

"With you becoming in my arms," Lady Chandra says. "With you breathing my breath and drinking my blood, everything changed. I didn't know that would happen, and even the seer didn't know that. She's not all-powerful. She's not infallible."

"So now we'll destroy her."

"She'll send things to destroy us," Lady Chandra says.

"I've been a hunter most my life."

"Now you're the hunted."

A grin forms on Nick's face that he's never felt before. It stretches at the ends of his lips and under his eyes in a way he's never experienced. It's a hungry grin. "They meant to watch me die in the arena."

"*I* meant to watch you die in the arena."

Nick takes a moment to respond. "You," he says, "I'll forgive."

There are more dogs. With their swords. Stupid silver blades. Even the proximity to their own weapons weakens them. Nick dives into them. Four this time. They slash at him. He slashes at them. His rips into the flesh. He tears limbs off the bodies. One of them nicks him with the blade. He saves that dog for last. The other three dead, still collapsing, holding their innards though there's nothing outside left to hold them in, he stands with one foot on the head of the last dog. One of its arms has been cracked in three places. Nick hardly remembers doing that. Instinct.

He looks at Lady Chandra. She hasn't gotten a drop of blood on her dress. That's as it should be. Nick Hunter has always stalked the night in search of prey. When he was human, mortal and alive, he preyed on the predators. Now that he's one of them, he sees no reason to change that. He'll destroyed everything in this mine, this shallow city, this Silver Blade. And then he'll return to the world, stronger and faster than he's ever been. He'll take the fight back to Richmond, first, and face the vampire there on equal terms. He never realized how lucky he had been to survive this long. Fortunate that his normal targets were the weaker, addled things that were left behind rather than the magnificent beasts typified by Lady Chandra and, yes, Jia Li, the vampire who had fought beside him and Jack Harlow a long time ago. Back when he was alive. He has such fond memories of living, but all of life now feels like his senses had been muted the whole time, like he'd been experiencing only a fraction of what he was experiencing.

He had only known bloodlust and murder and vengeance, not how deeply those emotions ran through him. Now he does. They're his essence. The very fiber of him. Every drop of blood, every muscle, every sinew, is infused with his need for it.

"The dogs," Lady Chandra tells him, "are fodder. To test your limits. Our limits."

"What else then?" Nick asks.

"Everything else."

He takes a deep breath and a good listen. He closes his eyes so as not to overwhelm his senses. Things move in the darkness, things so much of the darkness they simply are dark. He's seen them before. Wraiths and the like. He was mortal then. Easily frightened.

There's something in this chamber with them. Something made of folded shadows and smoke. The air chills so minutely, a mortal wouldn't have noticed until it was too late. He tells Lady Chandra with his eyes. He doesn't know what it sees or hears. It hasn't got organs like he does. It's not a man, or man-shaped, little more than mist.

"I've never seen a man I couldn't see," Nick whispers. He's circling the shadow, walking through it, trying to grasp it by taking it by surprise. He closes his fists so very slowly, a madman might go sane staring at them. The air has thickened. He doesn't move more slowly, but it takes more effort. It plans to choke him out. Freeze him solid. Encase him within a living shadow.

But he doesn't need breath and the cold doesn't bother him.

"There's something I've never seen," Nick says to Lady Chandra. "In all my hunting, I've never actually seen a transformation. Can I be a wolf, I wonder, or a bat?"

"You cannot," Lady Chandra says.

"Are you sure?" He has control over every cell, every molecule of him, how could he not manipulate his own body into whatever form he wants? He shifts. It's subtle, and subatomic, and painful. He endures the pain. He's suffered worse. The loss of his family, the loss of his mentor, the love of his partner and lover. Even the loss of his humanity, in the end. But he was a hunter, hardly a good example of the human animal. He's much better as a vampire. Instead of walking through the dark, he has swallowed it and contained it and embodied it.

Briefly, he looks in all directions at once. The outline of the shadow is clear to him now. It's not formless and without shape, but amorphous and malleable. Lady Chandra looks scared. He's never seen her scared before. He's known her all his vampire life, which is not so long a time. He's never seen a frightened vampire.

Bits of him drift away, like breath in the wind, drawn into the shadow. His sense of touch extends, but he's got to stop it. He's extending, but losing control and losing touch. What's lost is lost. The shadow consumes it. Transforms it. He thought to infiltrate the shadow, to overwhelm it, to disperse it, but instead it's pulling him apart at a molecular level.

Nick tries to draw himself back to himself, as best he can, wrestling for individual cells that were once part of his fingertips, his hair, his lips. He gouges the shadow, which is pointless. The shadow reforms over its own wounds. He inhales, taking in a breath of shadow and of his own shadow, as well as the mine and everything that's ever lived and died within it. The air around him is solid now, but like dirt, not rock. He pushes through it like a vampire rising from its grave. He likes the metaphor. It makes him grin. The grin reminds him of his strength. That strength pulses through every drop of blood and every drop of sweat. He inhales again, and now it's the shadow trying to pull away. The balance of their tug-of-war has changed. When he exhales, it's dead shadow, decaying bits of smoke, rancid and offensive.

The shadow ruptures.

The shadow bleeds. It's not blood, not human blood, but Nick drinks it anyway, drinks it deeply with an inhalation, absorbs all of the shadow. In his lungs, it's transformed. It feeds him, it gives him strength, it gives him life. And he expels the remnants. Purges it. He vomits black, shadowy mucus all over the floor of the mine. It's acidic, and burns through the floor, burns the metal of the cart rails, burns the dust of decades.

When he stands again, Nick Hunter takes a good, full breath of the stale mine air. Lady Chandra stares at him. Horrified and exhilarated. Her smile, tenuous at first, grows broad. "That," she says, "was magnificent."

"I'm a god now," Nick says. "A god of death."

Then, the strength is gone, and the poison of the shadow has infected him. His veins run cold and his muscles falter. Nick Hunter drops to his knees. He catches the side of the mine wall to stop his face from hitting the floor. He takes two, three gasping breaths of air, and says, "I need to feed."

3.

Naomi heals fast. She always has, especially when she can rest and focus on it. Vèt's variegated blood has helped. The wound still looks ugly and raw, but there's no fresh blood when she moves. It's not better, not by a long shot, but it's only her arm and she doesn't need it to stand.

Her legs, however, are weak. The healing has sapped all her strength. They hold her, but they don't make any promises.

Vèt speaks into the brazier, to the twin flames, the dancers. Naomi can see the how they're different than the fire around them, and how they're separate from each other. She's never seen sentient fire before, but there are lots of things she's never seen and lots of things she never will. Vèt steps aside, invites Naomi to converse with the dancers. It's dangerous to lean, but she does so. The heat is bearable because, as a girl in Haiti, there was always heat. She doesn't get close enough to burn. She whispers to them in Creole. They seem to respond to her voice. They flicker and shimmer. They have eyes, or the approximations of eyes. She tells them she respects them. She doesn't understand them, but she doesn't have to. The fires brighten. She takes a breath, primarily to hesitate, then apologizes for her role in delaying their birth. She pleads ignorance. She says she has known a wise man but hasn't yet achieved her own wisdom. She cannot read their responses. They pulsate, they burn more brightly, they turn away, they dance. She bows her head a moment longer, to show contrition, then stands upright again. The effort causes no pain, it merely requires strength. She steps toward Vèt's animals.

The three of them look back at her with big, expressive eyes full of expectation and even love. She's shocked to see it. Under the earth, in this *twou wòch nan fènwa*, this cave of darkness, she expected only violence and misery. She expected enemies at every turn, creatures that would devour her if given the chance. She expected to find Mr. Jack's hunter friend and leave.

But that was never the intention. They weren't brought here to save a hunter. They were sacrificed. Given to darkness.

She puts out her hands like she would for dogs, and she lets the beasts sniff at her and lick her hand. She turns to Vèt and says, "I'm weak."

Vèt smiles. She touches Naomi's lip with a finger, on which there's a drop of her blood, a deep indigo unlike the green visible under her skin. It's more than healant this time, but fortification. There's no time left to nurse her wounds.

Vèt takes a breath and says something in her language, something brilliant, no doubt, something inspiring. The dancers hop out of the brazier. The dogs shake themselves loose of each other and rise, powerful creatures with terrible jaws.

The remaining flames in the brazier go out. Darkness overtakes the cave behind them as they march. And they're not alone. Others in the dark walk with them, others who have gathered, who have been gathering, creatures and beasts and men.

Naomi doesn't know how she became part of this rising darkness. She doesn't know how she became a soldier in the coming war. She marches, just steps behind Vèt, their general and their queen.

It's the blood, of course. Vèt's blood, in all its colors, can be poisonous, acidic, or a healing salve. It might also act as a kind of zombie powder, giving Vèt control, or at least influence, over her victims. Suddenly, Naomi doesn't trust her own mind. She reaches into her pouch, pulls something restorative, a finely ground root, and slips a bit into her mouth. It tingles on her tongue and on the insides of her cheeks. She takes more and swallows it.

Still she walks. The weight of the creatures behind her urges her forward now. She may be doing the right thing, but she doesn't know, and that worries her. She should have been worried from the start. She should have taken something to end the pain before Vèt got her blood into her.

There must be two dozen creatures walking with her. They're not a legion, perhaps, but they're a force, but they're approaching the elevator shaft and suddenly even the size of that makes sense. No army can rise from the mines, not when they can only come up in small numbers. Vèt is leading these creatures to a slaughter.

There are dogs ahead, four of them, playing cards at a small table as they guard the elevator shaft. The cage itself isn't there. It's at the level above. Because the mines aren't designed to let things to escape. The mines are a prison.

The dogs are on their feet. Armed. Ready. And they're fodder. They don't stand a chance. They're variations of werewolves without the strength and cunning. They're brutes, but they're not particular effective as brutes. If they rely on numbers, four isn't high. These four pull their weapons and charge, but they're just charging into suicide. The creatures around Naomi now are not the twisted, degenerative castoffs rejected by the surface. They've been corralled because of the threat they pose. They were sent to the mines, to the shallow city of Silver Blade, to die and rot and be forgotten.

The dark does not die so easily, and it will never be forgotten.

One of the dogs is flayed in the amount of time it takes Naomi to draw a breath. Another is torn into pieces and savagely devoured. The third is thrown, bleeding and missing an arm, down the elevator shaft. The fourth is entirely disintegrated. Not even a whiff of ash remains.

Vèt, at the front of all this, turns and speaks to her army. She promises moonlight. She promises feasts.

4.

The Mayor's grin is all toothy and friendly like a shark's. He holds his hands out, palms up, as if to welcome Jack Harlow to the deep city. "How long to you intend to stay?"

"I don't."

"He's seen the stars," the scavenger says. "The real stars, up in the real sky, not just pearls and diamonds."

"Once, there were a hundred twisting paths to the surface," the Mayor says. "Most of them cut through the shallow city. As I said, those tunnels are being dealt with. Even now, there's a crew moving to demolish another."

"Do you plan to speak me to death?" Jack asked.

The Mayor laughed. "No, of course not. We knew you were coming. And we have something for you."

"You didn't know," the scavenger says. "I brought him. Nobody knew."

The Mayor locks his eyes on her. It's the first time he even acknowledges her, and she cowers under the intensity of it. But he speaks to Jack. "These caves have existed for thousands of years. Some of us were here when they built the mines and when they built the shallow city. Did you know they thought Silver Blade was haunted? By ghosts, no less. Have you seen many ghosts here, *DarkWalker?*"

There's weight to that word. It doesn't mean what Jack thought. The Mayor lets it hang in the silence, like a conductor holding the orchestra at a pause between notes. The scavenger shuffles her feet. Deep city sounds reach them, but the sounds are soft, muted, stealthy, as though everyone and everything in it stalks the city. The loudest sound, for a moment, is the continuous crashing of a waterfall not visible from this terrace.

The Mayor drops his voice to a whisper and leans close to Jack's ear. "Look again."

Ghosts. Jack sees ghosts. Spirits, phantoms, revenants, flickers, specters, and visions. They occupy all ends of the city. They're in the windows, in the streets, right here next to him. Some are faint, mere echoes of memory. Some are shrouded in gray or mist or obscurity. Some are practically physical. There are more varieties of ghosts, more distinctions, than Jack has ever known, and he's seen quite a few on the surface. Some are hideous, images of rotting, swelling corpses. Others are finely dressed, or not dressed at all, and all of them, every one, is dead.

"Our census taker says there are one hundred nineteen ghosts," the Mayor says, "but numbers like that fluctuate from time to time. And demons, *DarkWalker*? How many of those do you see?"

Demons, fiends, and devils occupy the city, as well. They live in big rooms atop the narrow buildings. They feed on trespassers and oathbreakers.

"I've seen demons more powerful than any of those," Jack says.

"Yes, yes, I'm sure you have. And what about the cave dwellers?"

"I'm a cave dweller," the scavenger says.

There are other kinds, other scavengers but also goblins, trolls, orcs, fiends with teeth and distorted countenances, bats that are half human or half monster, slithering things and crawling things darting through the streets of the deep city.

"You're not telling me anything I don't know," Jack says. "I've been hunted by creatures like these. I've been hounded by them all my life. I've been to hell, a dozen hells or more, and there's nothing you can do to impress me."

"Nothing?" the Mayor asks.

"Why do you need to be impressed?" the scavenger asks. "Shouldn't we just climb? Get out of here while we can?"

The Mayor shakes his head. "Come, *DarkWalker.*" Again with the pause. "Let me impress you."

He leads them down the wide steps toward the city proper. He winds through some of the streets, between the wraiths and ogres, up streets carved out of the rock like ancient European cities, where nothing's straight and nothing's level. He goes to a big red door, knocks three times, and pushes inside. Jack Harlow and the scavenger follow.

Pots and cauldrons and mason jars and perfume bottles fill the shelves that line the walls. An apothecary bends over a collection of roots and minerals. He's got tools out, and gloves on, but he pauses to look up. His crackled skin is jaundice yellow, his pale eyes filmed over, one ear entirely missing. When he speaks, it's with a voice never meant to speak. "Mayor?"

"Just passing through," the Mayor says. There's another door inside. The Mayor uses an iron key to unlock it. The mechanisms inside sound more formidable than any lock Jack's ever opened, but he has a way with locks and even this one would've obeyed him. On the other side, there's a narrow spiral stairway cut straight into the rock. They descend. It's tight and winding, the steps irregular and uneasy. As they descend, the Mayor speaks. "In the beginning," he says, "the caves were dug by giant rock worms, but no such thing exists anymore. They shit silver and sulfur and arsenic, and they left vast networks of trails and vast deposits of their shit." He laughs at that, as if it's a joke. "Some creatures, they need the darkness, the dryness or the dampness – every system of caves is unique. This system stretches a hundred miles in any direction. There are paths we have no desire to close."

The stairs continue downward. There's blood on the walls, where creatures have been slaughtered and where the rock itself has cried. Tendrils of metals snake through it like rivers on a map. Like stars in the sky.

"I didn't know this was here," the scavenger says.

"What would *you* know?" the Mayor asks. "*They* don't trust *scavengers* with secrets."

"Why trust me?" Jack asks.

"You should know."

The descent continues forever. No spiders crawl in the corners of this spiral stair. They do not walk through layers of dust or sediment. But no one comes down these stairs. The locking mechanism had wanted to resist the key. The air is stale, stagnant, dead. Even in the deep city, fresh air moves in and out.

"We have lived here, in one form or another, for all the length of memory," the Mayor says. The stairs end abruptly at another door. This time, the lock argues with the key, and the screech of it cuts the darkness like slow lightning. As the Mayor forces the door, the scavenger presses close to Jack's back. She reminds him of a woman he met in a city in hell, a one-eyed woman, a lost soul who found herself even in that infernal place.

A wave of heat rushes into the stairway. They enter a long, low-ceiling hall lined by pits of magma. Chains hang over the pits, and from those chains dangle skeletons no longer alive and skeletons still clinging to a sort of life. Pit masters stir the magma with large metal spoons. They sprinkle roots and rocks into the magma. It's like an oven here, intensely hot, and the corridor stretches two or three hundred years before reaching another doorway. The pit masters go about their work, never acknowledging the Mayor or his guests.

"Torture," the Mayor says, "or pleasure, depending on your proclivities."

The next doors requires no key. Two of the pit masters push the double doors open, revealing another large cavern, perhaps as large as the deep city or the lake above. A walkway runs the perimeter of the hole, but the slope is steep and long. At the bottom, half buried in mountainous piles of gold, is a dragon.

Jack Harlow has seen a dragon. Easily the size of a bus, it had passed over Orlando when he was vulnerable. He's no longer vulnerable, but he no longer feels strong, either. This dragon, with its metallic scales and sharp ridges and leathery wings curled underneath it, is as big as a stadium.

"He sleeps," the Mayor says. "He's slept for a thousand years. To really get the full effect of him, you need to see him in the air, flying, soaring, ripping apart the very fabric of reality. He's a dragon, yes, but he's not what you think."

"When will he wake?" Jack asks.

"When he wants to. Come." The Mayor walks around the perimeter, giving Jack and the scavenger plenty of time to gawk at the dragon. It's like trying to see the entirety of a skyscraper all at once; it's impossible. It's impressive.

"My momma used to tell stories of the dragons," the scavenger says. "She said they were big like elephants, but she could never tell me what an elephant was. She says there were three of them, once, roaming the countryside, and it took an entire tribe, all its warriors and women and children, all its history and all its potential, to bring them down and protect the land."

"I know the same story," the Mayor says. "They ripped the earth open and created the great river, and their bones are buried in the desert, waiting to be unearthed so they can be brought back again."

"I never believed it."

"Those stories," the Mayor says, "were true."

It's a long walk to the other side of the perimeter, where another set of doors is locked and chained and nailed shut. It's solid metal, heavy, lead and iron and chromium and titanium, alloys that defy description. Jack can sense the thickness of it, and the complexity of its locks.

The Mayor makes a show of pocketing the key. "I cannot open these locks. No one can. There's nothing more protected, more guarded, more contained than what's behind this door. There's nothing more dangerous, nothing more legendary – and yet the legends of it have withered. You might have heard whispers of its names, but those were never its names. You may have heard tales of its appetites, but no story could fully comprehend it."

"What's inside?" Jack asks. "Who?"

"The devil himself," the scavenger says, her voice a whisper.

"Nothing so superficial," the Mayor says.

"Who locked it – her – inside?" Jack asks.

The Mayor smiles. "She did."

The locks start to spin. The gears and cogs move. The layers of the locks unfold like onion skin, the strongest, hardest, densest, thickest onion skin imaginable. When one layer opens, it slides away, or rolls, or drops, and another series of locks begin to unfold. It moves slowly, loudly, and even the dragon behind them murmurs in its slumber.

"What's inside?" Jack asks again.

Another series of combinations unfurl. The thickness of the door is best measured in yards. Breathing can be heard from inside, terribly deep but strained breaths, lungs unused to drawing breath.

"Come," the Mayor says to the scavenger, putting a hand on her back. "You and I shouldn't be here for this."

Jack Harlow stares at the opening doors.

The scavenger resists for a moment, then turns and leaves with the Mayor. They walk swiftly. They walk around the perimeter, around the side of the sleeping dragon, so that Jack can meet what's on the other side of those doors alone.

"Is he safe?" the scavenger asks, looking back.

"None of us is," the Mayor says.

"What is it?" Jack asks again.

The Mayor pauses to look back. He's almost out of earshot. He's mostly swallowed by the gloom. But finally, he answers the question: "The *DarkWalker.*"

CHAPTER EIGHT

1.

Vèt's army gathers and grows. Naomi, near the front, wonders how many of these creature are under Vèt's influence and how many are there because they think it's a good idea. She speaks to her army, then turns to the elevator shaft, and Naomi's not sure what's going to happen.

Spiders. Spiders is what happens.

They crawl along the walls and ceiling, none of them any smaller than Naomi's hand, most with legs as long as her arms. As she watches, she draws from her pouch. She has nothing to counter the effects of Vèt's blood – there are too many possible effects and each would need its own remedy. And the creatures behind her, not just the spiders – what are they all, and what can they do?

The spiders climb the elevator shaft. They need no cage. They climb in a crisscross pattern, laying thick strands of silk, moving toward one side or the other to create a net for climbing.

Some of these creatures need no nets. Under other circumstances, at full health, Naomi could scale the walls – with the right tools, which of course she's got. She can't think about those right now. She'll have no need of them, and she has other, more pressing needs.

Vèt says something to her army. They're restless. They're eager. They're ready to fight. To conqueror. The night will be theirs, the shallow city of Silver Blade, the surface town, the valley, the mountain, the countryside, all united under one queen with green veins.

As a unit, the army starts to advance. Naomi goes with them, swept by the momentum, afraid of what might happen if she resists. She rubs a powder quickly over her eyelids to aid her vision in the dark. She swallows another, a restorative, hoping it'll clear the cloud in her mind. She has to do this slowly, surreptitiously, without deliberation. It's the nature of magic, that things take time.

But time is one of her magics.

She, along with others in Vèt's army, climbs the nets. They enter the elevator shaft and rise. The next level is high, and the effort reverberates painfully through her shoulder. The creature that gouged her is back there, one of Vèt's army, enslaved to the translucent woman's will. Beside her, there are vampires, werewolves, rats, reanimated corpses, beasts of every variety. Strong and numerous, they rise.

By the time Naomi reaches the highest level of the shallow city – the cage itself waits further above, on the same level as the adit, the Fox and the Silver Sparrow, and Lance Turner – she feels the heat in her blood when she thinks the name, and knows she'll soon feel the heat of his blood spitting from his arteries – by the time she reaches the level commanded by the seer, where she last saw Jack Harlow, the dogs guarding the elevator have already been slaughtered.

But the dogs were not alone.

Burke is among the other creatures, fully transformed into a ferocious and impossible version of a grizzly bear, crushing spiders and tearing into the flesh of the first arrivals. No one wears colors indicating loyalties. Some may be fighting just for the thrill of the fight.

She slips sideways through time, beyond the confines of this cavern, into the main room where nothing remains of the marketplace. It had all been an act. She slides again, into the seer's cavern.

Eulalia sneers at Naomi. She bears her teeth, human teeth under all her scars, and wields a short blade thick with poison. Naomi carries two blades of her own, short, curved around her hands, extensions of her fists. She says, "You don't have to die."

"Of course I do," Eulalia says.

"You don't have to die *today*," Naomi says.

Eulalia lunges forward, swinging the sword. She's slow, and easy to evade. She swings again. She's already resigned herself to death, or she wouldn't be here, in this room, defending her mistress.

Eulalia swings again, feigns one way and lunges. Naomi's not a supernaturally gifted warrior, but she doesn't need her powders to avoid that weapon. One strike may be enough to bring all sorts of things down. No single poison would work on all the beasts about to come at her.

Behind them, the fighting spreads beyond the elevator shaft. Vampires tear at vampires. Wolves rip apart dogs. The bear splits one thin creature in half.

Eulalia tries again.

"I'm not your enemy," Naomi says.

Eulalia sighs and lowers her sword. "I'm not a fighter."

"You should leave."

"There's only two ways out of the shallow city. The pits, or the elevator."

"Tania?"

"She's loving all this," Eulalia says.

"She knew this would happen?"

"She sees."

"You said she couldn't see the future."

"That may have been misleading."

Naomi glances backwards. The fighting will reach them soon. Tania's defenders are not so numerous as she might have expected. She asks, "Where's Jack Harlow?"

Eulalia smiles. It's a wicked, nasty smile, and it doesn't belong on the face of someone still human. "Gone."

Naomi lets that sink in. Absorbs it. Understands it thoroughly. *Gone* is not *dead*, but there's no way Tania would have let Jack Harlow out of this prison. That was the only reason they were here. "His friend? The hunter?"

"Changed."

That, also, is a weighted word. Naomi doesn't like it. She doesn't like Eulalia. She feels a great surge of hatred for the human girl. She pulls from her pouch.

"What are you doing?" Eulalia asks.

"Ending it."

"Ending what?"

"Silver Blade."

2.

Nick feasts on blood, the blood of dogs, the blood of succubi in the backmost rooms of the self-proclaimed queen. He gouges himself, and Lady Chandra watches with awe and admiration and fear.

"It's not enough," Nick says.

"It never will be."

"The blood is tainted. Their blood." Nick points at the succubus, sprawled all prettily on her silk sheets. He's hungry, he's starving, and there's nothing to eat, nothing good. "The queen, will she be fulfilling?"

"I became on the surface," Lady Chandra says.

"You had human blood." Nick winces at the word. He was human once, not so long ago. He hunted what he's become. He flexes his fists. His muscles ache and his stomach roils.

"And vampire."

"Feed me," Nick says.

The Lady Chandra had been transformed at a young age, and she's been a vampire half her life. She's young and inexperienced and not as strong as she should be. Nick sees this. He sees this, and the thirst is killing him. She offers her wrist. She's trying to be ladylike, whatever the hell that means. She wants to nurture him, but she can't. She's insignificant. He needs a real meal, a hearty feast, and she knows it as well as he.

He takes what she offers. A good swallow, a mouthful and another, easing the pain inside but not subduing it. It only delays the inevitable. He needs pure, fresh blood, not the stuff that flows through the veins of inbred animals scratching out a pitiable existence under the earth. He needs to see the moonlight and drink under the stars. It's not a compulsion, not a desire, not even a driving need. It's everything. *Everything.*

Lady Chandra snatches her arm away. "Enough!"

Nick licks a drop of blood from his lips. "Not even close."

Her blood has given him some strength, but it's insufficient. She's weak, because she subsists on what's on offer in this shallow city. He can't be that weak.

Lady Chandra says, "The seer has a human."

It takes a moment for Nick to realize she means the queen. He reaches out, exploring with his senses, smell and taste and hearing. The blood calls to him. Draws him. "Something's happening."

"You're still changing," she tells him.

"Not me. Something else. Something..." He doesn't know how to describe it, but there's blood being spilt. Lots of blood.

She detects it too.

He doesn't wait for her. He takes off down the corridor, heedless of what might lie ahead. He follows the scent. The aroma. The promise. He passes through a shadow. He passes one of the queen's female offerings, one of the brothel workers, without even seeing her. She's got blood, but it's insufficient, tasteless, pale, unappetizing.

The corridor leads to a large cavern at war.

Spiders, dogs, and bears. Wolfish things and human things, creatures of mist, mindless beasts, ripping each other apart, fighting with silver blades and claws and talons and razors and bludgeons. It's chaos.

Lady Chandra grabs his arm. "Don't," she says.

"So much blood."

Even dead things have died. A wash of blood coats the floor and walls and ceiling. There's a woman with translucent skin, green blood flowing through veins anyone can see. She's not fighting. She stands back and watches, and relishes the gore.

"Don't," Lady Chandra says again.

"I'm thirsty."

"She's stronger than us."

"Stronger than *you*." Nick breaks free of her grip, leaps over the fray, above the warring clans, straight for his target.

He throws her to the wall, tears into her throat before she can respond. The first mouthful of her blood is ecstatic, the purest pleasure he's ever felt. The second mouthful burns.

He pushes her away. Her veins run green, but the blood spilling from her throat is yellow and crimson and black. She says something nasty in a language Nick doesn't know and doesn't understand. Her blood courses through him and it burns. It ignites fires he never knew could exist. Did he drink acid? Poison? Death itself?

The woman sneers at him, and one of her pets, a big, amorphous thing with more teeth than physics should allow, roars. The cavern shakes at the sound of it.

Lady Chandra grabs Nick. He's not even sure what's happening anymore. The bear grabs Nick. He remembers the bear. Brian? Byron? Beck? Brock? He doesn't remember its name.

Nick Hunter spent his life hunting creatures like this. He never thought he'd become one. There's a moment in which he thinks, let them tear me apart. Let them rip me in half. I deserve nothing, no one deserves anything, and if I get out of here all I'm going to do is destroy hope and lives. I'm going to spread fear and death. I'm going to give in to these infernal instincts and drink my way through the whole of human society.

But those instincts have him. He resists death. He pulls the bear closer to him, the bear called Burke, and without a word, without a wry comment of any sort, he bites the bear's throat.

The bear's blood is good.

Lady Chandra pushes Nick – and the bear – back away from the fighting. The translucent woman is gone, the warring clans are gone, the shallow city is gone. They crash through the tunnel, cracking the rocks, shattering the timbers holding it all together.

The bear fights viciously. He throws the two vampires away from him. They're at the end of the tunnel, at the elevator shaft, and the cage is descending. The cage promises escape for any of the creatures here. Nick catches his breath, wipes blood from his jaw, and reasserts enough control to say, "Destroy that elevator."

The bear roars. The bear doesn't take orders, not from him. But the bear understands. The next swing of his mighty arms shatters wood and bends the rusting iron. The next swing of Nick's absurdly powerful arms shatters a lever. The Lady Chandra turns and faces the tunnel.

Nick knows a few things. He feels stronger than ever. The bear's blood, as little as he got, was fresh enough to clear his head, if only a little bit. He has no intention to die, no intention to surrender to the mine, to this city of Silver Blade, but he will not allow all the things down here to escape. He can save the upper world that much, at least.

He won't be able to kill the queen as he wanted. He'll never know what half of these things were. Jack Harlow, his friend who had come after him – there's no going back for him.

The cage continues to descend toward them. The real mechanisms are above, at the highest level, with the mine entrance. The cage descends, and it's not empty. There are men there, men with guns, men armed specifically to deal with what's down here. Six beating hearts pumping all that nourishing blood – but Nick's going to have to leave them. Let them do their damage. Let them burn through the beasts down here. Let them die, if they will.

He asks the bear, "Is there another way out?"

The bear grins. "No."

"We'll find a way," Lady Chandra says.

Nick grins. He's doing a lot of that now. He enjoys the power coursing through him now. He pulls Lady Chandra close and kisses her violently, passionately, bloodily. When they pull away, she's breathless, the bear has moved away from the elevator shaft, and the cage is close enough that the men with their guns are already taking aim. He whispers, so that only Lady Chandra can hear him. "The arena."

3.

Eulalia makes no move to stop her. Naomi tosses certain accelerants around her, lets them permeate the mine air and drift where they will. She recites words, old words but ones she understands, and spreads those, too, through the stagnant air.

Tania says, "This place was never meant to survive."

She stands at a doorway, draped in gold like the summer sun, the same dress she wore when Naomi first saw her. She's tall, her blonde hair an eternal cascade, her eyes green like Vèt's blood. Stepping through the doorway, she says, "I see you've met my sister."

"All this," Naomi asks, "is family drama?"

"It's much more than that. Look out there, look at those pathetic and terrible things, all these souls sealed forever in a manmade mine? How long did you think that would last?" Tania pushes Eulalia aside and stands face to face with Naomi. Like the queens of night and day, appearances be damned. "They're sending workers down now. Fresh fuel, you might say. Like you, but you were never going to be enough. We'll rise, all of us, out of this mine. I was its queen, but I was a queen of hollow dungeons and dust and dirt." She reaches out and touches Naomi's cheek. "You would do well in my brothel."

"They call you a seer," Naomi says, "but you can't see beyond what you've already seen, can you?"

Tania frowns. "Even now, as they fight out there, as they die in that cavern, as they sacrifice themselves for me, and for my sister, they're shaking the earth. They're calling to Jonathan Harlow and his watchers, inviting them to fix the problem they created. They're descending now. Not Jonathan himself, he will never return here. But they're sending their men, their fodder, who think they're ready to face what's been seething and growing down here." As if to punctuate the words, gunfire starts.

"Your mine is shot through with sulfur and its alloys," Naomi says. "Did you not see that?" She releases a spark, a single lick of flame from an eternal fire, a single spark to spread through the accelerants to the gases in the air, gases that have been building up and failing to ventilate for over a hundred years, and through those gases to the lines of sulfur – of brimstone – in the walls.

The flame moves fast. Like water, almost. It arcs through the air and ignites the veins of combustible alloys in the rock walls.

Briefly, Tania looks around, at the tiny flames spreading in all directions. She can see what's happening, what's about to happen, and there's fear on her face. Fear on Eulalia's face. To be fair, there's fear on Naomi's face, as well. She doesn't know how much time she has. She doesn't know how strong she is. She only knows she has to be fast, so she slips sideways, hard, through time itself, to flee the cavern and the creatures at war. She loses her footing in the blood, almost falls, manages to make her way to the tunnel that leads to the elevator. She glances back. Monsters killing monsters. Eulalia standing beside her seer, behind a thickening wall of molten sulfuric gases. The entire cavern brightens. Veins of sulfur, and sulfuric compounds, ignite in the walls and ceiling and ground, blue beads of fire all forming at once, spreading, seeping deep into the mine.

Naomi slips sideways again, down the shaft, to the elevator shaft, just as the cage itself is shattered and cut free of its cables by the bear, by Burke. She's glad to see him here. That means she doesn't have to hunt him on the surface. He sees her, but only briefly. There are soldiers, too, men in service of that organization, sent perhaps by Lance Turner, perhaps by Jonathon Harlow. She doesn't know and doesn't care. She takes a fraction of a second to slash Burke's throat. The wound won't kill him. She hasn't got time to do it properly. But it will prevent him from escaping.

Behind her, the sulfur, the blood, and the chemicals are combining and reacting. Her accelerants have taken hold. The air is being drawn into the mine, into the center of the explosion. Naomi cannot enjoy it from here. Another sideways slip, this time combined with climbing, doesn't give her as much advantage as she would like. Her shoulder bleeds afresh. Pain explodes out from it – razors tap dancing across her nerve endings.

Naomi reaches the top of the elevator shaft as the explosion takes hold. Vèt is there, emerging from the pit ahead of her. The translucent skin leaves her veins visible for all to see. She's emerging as if triumphant, barely aware of the explosion behind her, the explosion consuming her army and her sister's army.

Naomi's out of breath. Winded. She has to make one more run, but exhaustion is going to catch up to her. But she cannot let Vèt reach the surface. This is far enough. Fully in normal time, she and Vèt face each other as the world rumbles beneath them. The explosion sends up waves of heat and a horrible stench. The shockwave disrupts the footing of both Vèt and

Naomi, and it damages the mine from its deepest shaft to its mouth.

Protective measures, built into the walls, are active, but they have no effect on Naomi – she's not truly a creature of the night – and they have little effect on Vèt. The woman sees her, finally, and hisses, and curls her clawed fingers, and spits a stream of venom or acid or fire.

Naomi slides underneath, blades in her each hand, and slashes the woman's thighs. The femoral arteries are hard to miss in a woman whose veins are on display. Naomi's second slashes go for the calf muscles. Vèt spews her venom and screams her ancient curses. The damage is insufficient to kill. But that was never Naomi's intention.

Her last slash is at the front of the knees. Vèt stumbles back, her legs damaged and hurting and bleeding, the bones in her knees cracking. It's a step, half a step, but it's enough to send her over the edge of the elevator shaft, even as a second explosive wave bursts upward.

Naomi slides through time, one final push, using up all her reserves to get out of the mine of Silver Blade. A third underground explosion shakes the earth and the mountain and the aboveground town. She gulps the fresh air, struggles with disorientation, crumbles to the ground. The earth trembles again with a fourth explosion somewhere further distant.

She's only got strength enough to realize she's surrounded by armed men, and the barrels of all those military-grade weapons are aimed at the mine entrance and anything trying to escape it. The iron gate stands open, and its troll is nowhere to be seen. But it doesn't stand open for long. The mine collapses with a rush of smoke and dust and dirt and a few tendrils of flame.

From behind the men, one familiar man steps forward. He doesn't carry a weapon. It's Lance Turner, who brought them here to begin with, and he doesn't look very pleased. He kneels next to Naomi and offers a hand to help her stand. She wants to tear it off, but closes her eyes instead.

4.

In the center of the arena, alone with the undefeated, Nick Hunter and the Lady Chandra feel the power of the explosions, each in succession, but are spared the flames. The ceiling, however, cracks, and drops huge chunks of rock and dirt. It's a high, natural ceiling, and it won't come down easily – but it will come down.

But not on them. They leap, high as they can, together, for the highest point of the ceiling. They reach it, and they catch it, and they dangle there a moment before burrowing upward, into the weakened, disturbed dirt. Together, they dig and they claw their way through the ground. When the way is rocky, they work around it, they work through it, they pulverize what they're able, and they do not stop.

It's a long, hard, arduous climb, but the grounds around Silver Blade have shifted, so ascension is possible.

No one's there to see their hands break free of the dirt in the mountainous forest. No one sees the two vampires rise from their graves. But they rise, and they're hungry, and Nick Hunter has an idea of where they can go. They'll catch a meal along the way.

5.

Several creatures try to escape the explosions by leaping into pits. At the bottom of one of those pits is only spikes of silver and iron and other metals, and death may be a long time in coming. At the bottom of another is nothing, so when the ceiling collapses there's no place to run. At the bottom of one of the longest, deepest falls, is a massive lake, around which scavengers watch as debris and bodies tumble into their realm. But they won't move to salvage anything, not yet, because the lake creatures are all astir, and their tentacles and claws and stingers and stalks dance across the surface of a usually still lake. The lake creatures do their own bit of salvaging, dragging down the creatures that tried to escape the flames. The sulfur fires burn for a long time, but they will burn themselves out. When the do, the lake will go still again, and the creatures beneath its surface will sleep again, or rest, or wait, or whatever it is they do.

6.

Under the mine, and under the shallow city of Silver Blade, in the deep city, the scavenger looks up as the sky – not a sky, but a rock ceiling high above them – trembles and drops dust. "Will we die?" she asks the Mayor.

"One day," the Mayor says, also looking up. The caves beneath the shallow city were there long before men dug out their mines. The caves beneath the shallow city will still be there tomorrow. And the deep city will not disappear. Yet.

7.

Deeper still, the distant rumblings do not disturb the dragon. The dragon's a creature of brimstone and hellfire. The little fires of men mean nothing to it.

8.

In the vault, Jack Harlow, DarkWalker, faces one of his own.

She's older than dirt, older than the mine and older than these caves, possibly as old as the earth itself. Her skull isn't quite the same shape. Her eyes are narrower, her lips larger, her ears flattened. The wrinkles are impressive, but the skin isn't flesh anymore, it's something rougher and dry as chalk. Her color is off, too, a slight yellow, though that could be the lack of light. She smiles, but it's hardly recognizable. She lays on a divan carved out of the rock. The chamber is not as big as might be expected, but it contains a dozen shelves full of books, an old phonograph machine on a table, an assortment of paintings on the wall, though some have faded so much there's nothing visible but the suggestion of an image. A record is playing, a symphony playing something Jack recognizes but doesn't know. The recording sounds distant, the scratches and dirt on the record much closer.

She beckons him closer. "Let me look at you," she says. Her voice is as old as she is. Her accent is impossible to place because it belongs to a civilization not just lost but utterly forgotten.

Hesitantly, Jack approaches. "I don't understand."

She takes a deep breath, looks at the wall, the unlit candle on the desk, then to Jack. "You're young," she says. "You'll learn."

"What's your name?"

"Eve."

"As in Adam and...?"

"Don't be ridiculous." She looks him up and down. "You're so full of questions, but you're not used to asking them, are you? Don't answer that. You're not used to answering them, either. I don't know how you managed to live this long. Oh." Her eyebrows go up. "Your parents, your sister, all watchers. So you caught that first."

"I'm not following you," Jack says.

She shakes her head. "You know what you are, don't you?" When he doesn't immediately respond, she says, "You can answer that."

"I do."

"I know. I see it on the tip of your mind. At the top, floating there, an identity without definition."

"I'm a DarkWalker," he says.

She smiles. "DarkWalker? Is that how it's said now. It was *wælgeuga* last time I heard it."

"Still DarkWalker."

"I forget. It's been so very long. His name was...I forget his name. Do you care? You don't. Good. He was a bright boy, but a boy, and he died. He never understood what he was. Feared it. He learned fear of himself, but you haven't. I don't know if that's good. Do you think it's a good thing, not to fear oneself?"

"I don't know."

"You're young," she says. "You're not supposed to know. He was so full of fear. That the church would catch him. Burn him. Something. I don't remember. Tell me, young DarkWalker, how do you feel?"

"I don't know what you mean."

"Do you feel strong, next to me?" she asks. "Do you feel old? I am, you know. Very, very old. But I'm not as old as the mountains." She chuckles. It's a dry, vacuous laugh, and it's got no resonance. "Not all of them. I sleep, sometimes. I miss years at a time. I collect sounds and colors and words, and I listen to them and drink them and bathe in them." She smiles again. "I'm older than this language."

"I can't speak any others," Jack says.

"You can, you just choose not to." She shakes her head. "Why are you here?"

"I'm not sure."

"You must know."

"I was led here. By the Mayor."

"Is that what it's called now?" Another shake of the head. She looks brittle, fragile, breakable, like every motion might be the last that ends in collapse and dust. "Why are you here?"

"To learn?"

She makes a dismissive sound with her tongue. It's unique to her. He's never heard it before, but he understands the tone. "What did you say you were?"

"Jack Harlow."

"I don't care. I'll forget your name, too, eventually."

"DarkWalker."

"I was a DarkWalker before you were born, before your parents were born, before your civilization was born, before your *species* was born. You're not unique, DarkWalker. Do you know that? Did you think you were?"

"I've never met another."

"There are no others."

"Why is that?"

"There are gods enough," Eve says. She takes a deep breath. Holds it a moment. "Gods enough."

"Why are you here?" Jack asks.

"Same reason as you," she says. "This is a prison."

"A prison to hold you?"

"I built it myself," she says. "What do you think?"

He doesn't answer that. He doesn't know what he thinks. He's not a thinking man. He doesn't spend a lot of time considering or pondering or conferring or conversing. He's read books but never studied them. He doesn't have opinions. For a long time, he didn't even act. He moved from place to place seeking solace and refuge and quiet.

"That's it, precisely," she says. "Solace. Refuge. Quiet."

"You can read my mind?"

Another dismissive click. "Don't be ridiculous."

"Why am I here?" Jack asks.

"Fools. Idiots. Madmen. Take your pick. Someone wants to contain you."

"Why are they fools?"

"You cannot be contained," Eve says. She leans forward. Her bones creak as she does. Her eyes are the color of sulfur. "Come closer, DarkWalker, let me look at you."

"How good are your eyes?" Jack asks.

"I don't mean to look with just my eyes."

He steps closer. She puts a hand on his chest. It's like a rock, as heavy as a mountain, fingernails like diamonds. Another hand on his forehead. The skin is rough and sharp, and it cuts him.

"I'm old," she whispers. "I've broken and built empires, I've crushed cities to rubble and burnt them to ash. I've fucked gods, DarkWalker, and I've been to the moon. Do you believe me?"

"Yes."

"You should. But I'm a liar." She laughs again. "And you, you're a DarkWalker. You're still young. Weak. But stronger than you know." She climbs to her feet. A chain, a thin silver chain wrapped around her waist, ties her to the rock, but Jack knows it's entirely for show. No chain, no thickness of chain, no amount of magic could hold her in place. When she moves, the rest of the planet moves with her, as though she dances with the world. The scraping of bones under her skin sounds like heavy concrete blocks dragged across each other. "I'm going to give you something, DarkWalker. You won't understand and you won't enjoy it, not right away, but you will." She has him by the back of the head and the waist now, and he cannot pull away as she kisses him. It's a long, brutal, soulful kiss, complete with memories not his and the scents of fields of jasmine and vanilla, the sounds of instruments lighter and airier than flutes, more ethereal than violins.

When she pulls back, she looks younger. More vibrant. There's color in her cheeks, and the sulfur in her eyes has been replaced by fire opals, brilliant orange and green and red in a sea of obsidian black. She doesn't let go, and keeps her voice at a whisper. "I don't know what I gave you, not precisely. A little bit of everything, I presume. Because that's what you are. DarkWalker. It's never meant what you thought. What they thought. They put you in a hole in the ground and thought that might contain you. They didn't know. You didn't know. So young." She shakes her head one last time. "Turn the record over for me."

Jack hadn't noticed it had ended. He walks to it, removes the needle, flips the record. The writing on the disc is illegible. He sets the needle carefully at the beginning of the next orchestral piece.

When the music begins, Eve says, "It's been nice, this visit. I do hope you'll visit again one day. When you haven't got so many questions."

"Have you answered any of them?" Jack asks.

"I'm sure I have." She smiles, and sits again. She closes her eyes and leans back on the earth divan. She's so perfectly still, Jack isn't even sure she's alive. He says her name, he wants to ask another question even if he doesn't know which one. She offers no response. She might be the rock itself, the minerals, the dirt and metal in the earth. She might be the earth. She might have lied.

Jack Harlow steps out of the vault. The doors start closing again, reengaging their complicated locks. The last strains of music are already fading.

He walks deeper into the earth, away from the deep city of Silver Blade, which was flourishing even when men burrowed into the earth to make the shallow city. Maybe they knew what they were doing, but probably not.

The earth swallows Jack Harlow. But there are miles of tunnels twisting through the rock, and eventually, without error, the DarkWalker emerges into the moonlit night. The air is fresh and vivid with night scents, brilliant with them, and brighter than he's ever seen.

EPILOGUE

1.

Nick Hunter is still what he always was. He's thirsty, he's thirsty all the time because he was made wrong, he was made in the dark, with insufficient oxygen and tainted blood and all the wrong minerals. The Lady Chandra accompanies him. She's afraid of him now. She fears for her life. Her immortality. They go first to Richmond, Virginia, where Nick's last hunt had been interrupted.

2.

Jonathan Harlow and his organization – or his organizations, it's hard to keep track of them – took over the city of Silver Blade many years ago and made it into something it never had been, something it had never been meant to be. The experiment, if it could be called that, didn't work. They keep other secrets, too, but Jack Harlow isn't interested in their secrets. He isn't interested in their knowledge. He doesn't want to know what they know or how they know it. They've treated him badly from the start, from birth, and now they've got one of his friends.

He doesn't intend to expose their secrets. He intends to destroy them.

COMING SOON:

DARKWALKER 4
ARMAGEDDON

NOTES AND ACKNOWLEDGMENTS

Thanks to everyone who read *DarkWalker*,
enjoyed it, reviewed it, criticized it,
and threw it across the room.
I promise this will only get stranger.

Special thanks for the continued support of
Mery-et Lescher. None of these happen without you.

Thanks, also, to Brent Tiano,
as this was written in the cave;
to all my First Readers on all my projects;
the Five Horsemen (Mike, Mikey, Coop, Brian);
my various inspirations;
anyone who has ever taught me anything;
the ghost of Edgar Allan Poe;
and my Mom.

I have missed people. I always do. I am so sorry.

And as always: Sabine and the Rose Fairy.

ABOUT THE AUTHOR

John Urbancik was born
on a small island in the northeast
United States called Manhattan
at the dawn of a terrible and terrific decade
and grew up primarily on Long Island,
but he has lived in Florida, Virginia, and Australia.

His first novel, *Sins of Blood and Stone*,
came out in 2002.

DarkWalker was originally published
in 2012 as the first of a series.
The rest of the series has remained hidden.
Until now.

John Urbancik also hosts a podcast, InkStains,
based on his writing project of the same name.

www.DarkFluidity.com